ESTHER

NORAH LOFTS

LARGE
PRINT

First published in Great Britain 1951
by
Michael Joseph

First Isis Edition
published 2018
by arrangement with
the author's estate

A catalogue record for this book is available
from the British Library.

ISBN 978–1–78541–525–8 (hb)
ISBN 978–1–78541–531–9 (pb)

Published by
F. A. Thorpe (Publishing)
Anstey, Leicestershire

Set by Words & Graphics Ltd.
Anstey, Leicestershire
Printed and bound in Great Britain by
T. J. International Ltd., Padstow, Cornwall

This book is printed on acid-free paper

Artaxerxes, K
the one girl v
passed over: a
streets of his
the chattering
this changelin
Queen of Per
soon loses he
hide her faith
the King's fa
enemy of the
Esther's only
own life and
already dispos

CHAPTER
ONE

All the garden of the palace of Shushan was washed in moonlight and looked as though it were made of ebony and ivory, so white lay the light on the bleached grass and on the marble pavements, so black were the yews and the shadows they cast. On such a night, as a rule, one could look out from the steps of the south side of the palace and see straight across the patterned black and white garden to where the fountains played, throwing up their silver, but to-night between the palace and the fountains loomed an immense dark shadow.

Artaxerxes, looking from habit towards the fountains, paused at the top of the palace steps and said abruptly: "We shall need torches in the pavilion. Forty at least. The Queen has not seen the place yet and I want her to see it at its best."

There was no sign of haste or urgency in the demeanour of the servant who took the order, yet within the space of five minutes twenty young Nubian boys, black as the yew shadows and wearing loincloths as white as the marble they trod, went racing across the garden; each bearing two torches whose flames streamed backward, and whose smoke gave off the aromatic scent of pine.

Artaxerxes tapped his foot and sighed and examined his nails as though he hoped that one of the ten of them would offer him some entertainment during the time of waiting. He had made the usual allowance for female dilatoriness and come late to the place of meeting, but even so he must wait. Vashti, he thought, with an impatience touched by tolerance, must be having difficulty in deciding between diamond earrings or pearl ones, or trying out a new way of dressing her hair for to-morrow.

And then suddenly he was conscious of the scent of roses, and a hand, light as a feather, was laid upon his arm, and a voice light, unapologetic, amused, asked, "Have I kept you waiting?"

"Not to matter," he said indulgently, "but I ordered torches, not lamps, and the little fiends ran so hard with them, racing one another I suppose, that they'll be half burned out before we get there unless we hurry." And he added the words that he had already spoken to his attendant, only this time with a certain wistfulness: "I wanted you to see the place at its best."

"Come along then, why are we waiting?" Vashti asked and began to move lightly down the steps. He allowed her to precede him a little, for he enjoyed watching her. She had a grace of movement that was, the King thought, unmatched amongst women, and he liked to look at her when she was not looking at him; he hated to admit it, even to himself, but there was a cool, slightly mocking quality about her gaze which made him feel uncomfortable, and there were times when he had to remind himself that *he* was King of Persia and that Vashti was only its Queen, and only its Queen because he had chosen to marry her out of all the women in the world. So now he followed a pace or two behind her and stared his fill at her slender upright figure in its fluttering gauzy robe, and at the proud carriage of her head where the jewels glittered in her copper hair. At the foot of the stairs, however, she halted and he caught her by the hand and urged her forward. There was something in his attitude of the little boy who has discovered something of immense interest to him which he is anxious to share with an approving grown-up. And with something of a grown-up's condescending patience the Queen of Persia allowed herself to be hurried across the garden and into the great pavilion which reared its dark bulk between the palace and the fountains.

The little Nubian boys had arranged themselves well. Against the taut-stretched, many-coloured, silken walls of the immense tent they stood like statues, evenly spaced, motionless. They might have been ebony figures designed for the holding of torches. And the torches had steadied down after their flight across the garden and were burning with a clear, steady light. Artaxerxes halted his Queen at the entrance and looked round a little anxiously and then with gathering confidence. It was beautiful, he thought, and it was magnificent. It was unprecedented, too. No other King or potentate that he had ever heard of had ever had the idea of giving such a feast that the guests must be accommodated outside his palace, and no other temporary building had ever been erected on such a splendid scale, with such complete disregard for cost, with such taste.

With such taste . . . the words lingered in his mind as he looked round upon the pavilion capable of seating three thousand guests in luxurious comfort. The pillars which supported the structure were all of silver or gold or marble, and stretched from pillar to pillar and making the whole ceiling were lengths of silk, white and blue and green and purple. Of the purple he was especially proud, for such a colour never came out of a Persian dye vat. It was the product of Tyre, and was obtained from the crushed bodies of a sea mollusc that was dredged out of the sea by myriads of slaves. It was beyond all description costly, especially when it had to be transported so far inland, and of all the furnishing of the pavilion — save one only — Artaxerxes was most proud of that purple silk. Not that the rest was not impressive enough. There were the long low tables of ivory and ebony and cedar wood; and flanking them innumerable couches with frames of silver and gold and cushions of the same silk as the walls; and set out in readiness for the feast to-morrow were all the dishes and drinking vessels, all solid silver or gold, and many of them encrusted with jewels which winked and glittered in the torch light. Artaxerxes thought, with some justification, that never had such a sight greeted any mortal eye, and he waited for some word of astonishment to break from Vashti's lips.

4

None came. Very, very slowly the Queen took in the whole scene, lifting her grey-green eyes with their artificially darkened lashes to the roof, where in the centre of the huge dome a great ornament, blindingly bright with gems, hung, and then letting them travel slowly, how slowly, over the walls and the tables and the couches and the gold and silver vessels. Finally her gaze travelled to the floor, which had been paved in marble, red and white and black, laid out in intricate patterns. For one wild optimistic moment Artaxerxes imagined that he had impressed her so much that she was speechless. He waited. And then Vashti said, in the sweetest, lightest voice: "I wish you had asked me to help you, Artaxerxes. I would, you know, willingly. I could have advised you about the colours."

"The colours?"

"The colours," she repeated in a firm voice. "So gaudy. All that purple! With red in the floor. Ah yes, yes, I know," she said, hastening to forestall a remark which would never have occurred to him in his dismay, "one can grow purple lilies and red together, the fuchsia even puts the two colours together on the same flower, but what is right for nature is often wrong for art. The white and the blue — see, over there, that stretch between the boy with the hair in his eyes and the boy with the thin legs, see — that piece, with the white and blue and the green in the floor is lovely, but the rest is hideous. Darling, I think you had better open your feast with a speech and admit that you're quite colour blind. That will sound very lovable." She laughed, an entrancing amused tinkle that had often

5

made Artaxerxes think of bells chiming. And, without noticing the expression on his face, she went on: "People like to think that the great have their weaknesses. Think how comforting it will be to all these conquered kings and princes and ambassadors and satraps, or whatever you call them, to think that the great King of Persia is colour blind."

"They aren't being brought here to think things like that," Artaxerxes said in a grating voice. "They're coming because they *are* conquered kings and princes, and I want them to see the might and the glory of Persia which conquered them. I mean to show them . . ." A thought flashed into his head and he snatched her hand: "Come here. Look at this. On the top table of all. What do you think of that?"

He dragged her towards the table at which, on the morrow, he would sit with his specially chosen, specially favoured guests. Set out upon this table, which was of ivory inlaid with coral and silver, were some vessels of unusual shape and design, very plain, very solid, lacking the ornamentation of rams' heads and bulls' torsos and twining flowers and foliage which was customary. Vashti looked at them for a moment in silence and then said: "This is the table where you will sit, Artaxerxes."

"Yes," he said.

"And like an ideal host you have kept the plainest vessels for your own use. How unlike you."

"They are very special," he said, and lifted a silver candlestick and turned it thoughtfully about in his hands. "Do you know what these are?"

She shook her head.

"These are the altar vessels of that god of the Jews. Brought from Jerusalem. D'you remember, Nebuchadnezzar sacked that city and then we sacked Babylon. Nobody knew what they were, and they were so plain and so heavy that they weren't considered suitable for palace use and found their way into one of the kitchens. And then one day an old Jew . . . wait a moment, I can't remember his name it was so very outlandish . . . came into the kitchen for something or other and saw them and began to weep and tear his clothes — not that they needed much tearing, I'm told. And they asked him what was wrong, and he said that these were the vessels of the most high god, Jehovah, especially made for religious purposes and very, very holy. One of the servants brought the old man and a cup or two up to me, and the old man explained all about them. Quite interesting it was. And I saw that . . . oh, probably you'll think this very fanciful, my dear," he said, aware again of the cool mockery in her gaze, but determined to finish his explanation, "I saw that, in a way, these things were more precious than that silver gilt stuff from Nineveh, or the set of tableware Pharaoh gave me when I visited him . . . because these have significance. They have a history. Solomon ordered them you know . . . the great Solomon." He looked into Vashti's face, eager for some response, found none and continued rather flatly, "Anyhow, I thought I would use them to-morrow just to show." He paused, not quite certain what words to use. "After all, the Jews were a great nation, and in conquering *their* conqueror we conquered them. And using their holy vessels at a feast will be *significant*."

But even as he spoke he knew that he had failed, failed for the thousandth time, to impress her. A little feeling of anger snaked through his sense of failure. After all, he was King of Persia and Lord of one hundred and twenty-seven provinces, master of an empire which stretched from India to Ethiopia, the like of which had never been seen before. And though he was an upstart — he had only been upon the throne for three years — she had upheld and increased Persia's might. Times were strange and upheavals were general; Vashti might pride herself upon her race and her family ... but what did that count? Her father had been defeated in battle and but for the fact that he, Artaxerxes, had looked on her with favour and made her his wife she might now be living a life of genteel poverty in a ruined palace far away in the wilds, selling her jewels one by one to Arab hucksters, never having a new robe. She might remember that — he thought — and give a man his due. She might now, at this moment, for example, say something about how splendid it was for a man to have upon his table the vessels dedicated to the service of a god, however rural and queer and ineffective that god might be.

But Vashti turned from the table and said, "I never liked Jews."

"Nor did I," Artaxerxes found himself hastening to say. "I never could stomach all that talk about being a Chosen People; and so mercenary, too. And yet . . ." an essential honesty within him came to the surface, "I

8

rather liked that old man. Its difficult to explain, he was ragged, but so clean, and he had been crying and his eyes were red, but he was sincere. That was it . . ." The man who was King of Persia and Lord of all the land between India and Ethiopia lifted his head and his eyes took on a remembering look. "He was sincere. It was from his heart he spoke when he told me, me, that though Jehovah's candlestick might stand in my kitchen, I was not fit to stand before Jehovah's feet."

"Did he say that?" Vashti asked. "I would have cut off his head."

"I just laughed and dismissed him," Artaxerxes said.

Vashti smiled as though to say, you would. And then, with the graciousness which she occasionally showed, stretched out her hand. "About these colours . . . come and see what I have arranged for to-morrow."

They left the pavilion and the little Nubians thankfully doused the torches, which were beginning to burn dangerously low and near the fingers. Vashti had not suggested building a special pavilion for her guests — the wives and daughters and consorts of the men who would attend Artaxerxes' feast. Instead she had thrown the whole of the women's part of the palace into one by opening doors and screens and, where necessary, cutting whole walls away. And a feeling of unity had been given to the diverse apartments by the hangings of pale rose colour. Every wall was hung, every cushion covered in the same colour. Here and there curtains were looped back or cushions bound at their edges with cords of a deeper shade of the same colour, and all the floors were covered with silky carpets of the deeper shade.

"This has significance too," Vashti said, emphasising the word to show that she remembered Artaxerxes' remark about the vessels that came from Jerusalem. "Rose is the colour of Petra. It is known as the rose-red city, you know."

There was nothing in the least offensive about that sentence, there was nothing insulting about the voice in which it was uttered; but Artaxerxes winced, for it reminded him that Vashti was a Princess of long lineage, that Petra had been a city known to the world before one stone had been laid upon another in Shushan. And it reminded him, most hurtfully of all, that his Queen whom he thought the most beautiful woman upon earth, neither respected nor loved him. If she respected him she would not dare to say such things, and if she loved him she would have understood how much they hurt.

"Sleep well," he said, as they reached the door of her private apartment. "The first guests will arrive early to-morrow. Good night."

"Good night," she said graciously. And then, as though by an afterthought: "If you repent of that purple, Artaxerxes, I have rolls and rolls of the rose-colour left. It would blend better and it would take no more than an hour to change."

"I don't think," he said gravely, "that it is worth the trouble. My guests will be men, and our teeth are not so easily set on edge. But I thank you for the thought. Good night."

10

He turned his steps towards his own apartments and then changed his mind. That purple, *was* it so offensive? It was strange, he thought, the effect which Vashti had upon him. He'd been too much taken aback by her criticism to say, "But purple is the royal colour, the colour of kings!" That was what he should have said. That would have silenced her. That would have reminded her that he was King of Persia. He was King of Persia, and to-morrow three thousand kings and princes and ambassadors, satellites and tributaries and sycophants were coming to the feast to which he had bidden them. He was the greatest potentate in the whole world . . . and a woman had called him colour blind.

He shouted loudly for a torch bearer, and within a minute a young man appeared bearing a torch in either hand. He was not one of the Nubians, his skin was the colour of pale honey, and his black hair sleek as silk. His face, as he turned it towards his master, mutely inquiring whither he desired the torch carried, wore a look of alertness and intelligence that was only just short of arrogance.

"To the pavilion," Artaxerxes said, answering the look, and the young man lighted the way.

In the small radiance of one torch where twenty had flared, the size of the pavilion was emphasised, the colour diminished. Artaxerxes signed to the young man to walk ahead, and together they circled the vast tent. Whenever the torch light struck upon a place where the purple met the red, Artaxerxes paused and considered the combination. It seemed to him entirely unoffensive.

His anxiety about the colours lessened and his uneasiness about Vashti increased. Had she intended deliberately to hurt him, to make his preparations seem ridiculous, to undermine his self-esteem? And if so, why? What had he ever done to hurt her? He had brought her out of half-ruined Petra and set her on the throne of Persia. He had never denied her anything; always treated her with respect. Why should she look on his preparations for the feast which was the celebration of his three years' reign, the peak of his life so far, and try to find fault with them; comparing Shushan — without actually saying so — unfavourably with that dirty, meagre city that consisted mainly of caves in the rock, Petra? Why?

A gulping sound made him look round. He perceived with some surprise that his torch-bearer had tears running down over his high-boned cheeks.

"Why do you cry?" he asked, suddenly kind because he felt, truth to tell, so like crying himself.

"It is all so beautiful," the young man said, tossing his head so that the tears flew to left and right of him in the torchlight. My Lord, it is all so beautiful and so magnificent that I cannot restrain my tears.

"Your perception does you credit," said Artaxerxes a trifle harshly, for he was not accustomed to exhibitions of emotion from his menials, "but what do you think of this, eh? Look at that purple against the red. What do you think of that?" He put his hand on the young man's arm and forced the torch forward so that its light shone on a place where the purple of the curtain met the red of the pavement.

"That, my Lord, is the royal purple triumphing over the blood of its enemies," said the torch-bearer.

"You are a poet, boy," said Artaxerxes, not very kindly. "And this, what do you make of this?" He twisted the torch so that the light fell upon the sacred vessels from the Temple at Jerusalem.

"It is the truth you seek?" the young man asked, and his voice was suddenly the voice of one who addresses an equal. Artaxerxes nodded.

"My Lord, I am an Amalekite. We are a small people, but for many years we fought the Jews and we had our successes. And our failures. I rejoice to see the symbols, the vessels of the false god of our enemies, put to their rightful purpose, the glorification of the King who has no equal upon this earth." The eyes of the young man were dry now, and glittered as he spoke.

"These feuds die hard," Artaxerxes said thoughtfully. "But you speak well. A well-oiled tongue hangs in that head of yours. To-morrow you shall serve the wine at this, my own table, and out of these vessels too. Have you ever served at a feast?"

The young torch-bearer shook his head "No, my Lord. I have but just entered the palace service.

"Then I will instruct you. Press no man to drink, but be vigilant. As soon as a cup is empty be there at the guest's elbow, ready to serve. Be watchful for the dregs and empty them away. I can think of nothing more to tell you, but there you are . . . instructed by the King himself."

"You do me great honour, my Lord."

"And you explained to me the significance of purple upon red. I shall remember that. What is your name, boy?"

"My name is Haman, my Lord."

"Haman. I shall remember that too," said Artaxerxes and straightway forgot it. But at the back of his mind there lurked the memory of the young man who had restored his self-esteem and flattered his vanity.

CHAPTER
TWO

By the seventh evening, though no one would have dreamed of admitting it, the feast had lasted too long. Host and guests had passed from pleasure to satiety; there had been too much to eat, too much to drink, and too many diverse entertainments. Artaxerxes had sat through the last and most sumptuous banquet of all with a gathering feeling of biliousness and flatness which even the arrival of a troupe of Indian dancing girls did little to relieve. He cursed the queasiness of his stomach, blaming it for his inexplicable depression. The whole affair had been an unquestioned, a dazzling success, everything had gone perfectly until now; and the arrival of the dancing girls should have marked the climax, the absolute zenith of a feast which had never been equalled. For the girls were not only beautiful and skilled — they were something that had never been seen in Persia or any part of the Western world before; Artaxerxes' guests were enjoying something quite unique. And, moreover, the girls represented something. The immensity of the Persian Empire, which reached out its tentacles so far that it could touch India and dredge even that distant country for ten minutes' entertainment.

This fact was not lost upon the guests, who as soon as the display was over, crowded about their host with flattering and complimentary speeches which he received graciously, though with little pleasure. I would have liked — he thought sourly — to have shown them something that would have reduced them to utter speechlessness; I've heard the words "magnificent," "overwhelming," "splendid," "incredible," so often that they have lost their value. I'd like to show them something that would stun them into silence.

But he could think of nothing further. He had displayed everything he owned — his jewels, his palace, his wonderful menagerie of wild beasts brought from every corner of the earth, his black slaves from Nubia, his white ones from the Caucasus; his strange gladiators from the far cold North, immense, hardly human men who wore nothing but a loincloth made of skin, and who fought with wild beasts or with one another less as a profession than a pastime. He had nothing left to show.

Talk at the King's table, originating with comments upon the unusual form of the Indian girls' beauty, swung over into discussion of beauty in general and hardened down into an argument as to which were the most beautiful women in the world. As a change from being entertained conversation was welcome, and the arguments became heated, with one man advancing the claims of Egyptian women, another Greek, another, with intent to flatter Artaxerxes, saying Persian, and one bold fellow admitting that the loveliest woman he

16

ever saw was a Jewish shepherd girl keeping sheep outside desolate, sacked Samaria.

Suddenly something flashed into Artaxerxes' mind, the great boredom lifted, and even the queasy stomach quietened. There was the thing he owned, the most beautiful and most precious of his treasures which these clacking fools had not yet seen. How could he have been so stupid as to think, a moment since, that he had nothing further to display. He turned to his guests and with renewed good humour, said:

"My noble friends, here is one argument that I can settle at once. Not one of you has mentioned Petra as the place that produces the most beautiful women on earth, but I think that in a moment you will agree with me that it does. For it has done so." He raised a finger and the watchful Haman stepped forward. "Boy, run over to the Queen's apartment and warn her to put on her best robe and the royal crown if she is not already wearing it — it is a trifle heavy for ordinary wear. Tell her that in five minutes the chamberlains will come to escort her here. Run now."

Haman ran. Slaves began to move about the pavilion with flagons of fresh wine; three harpists played sweet music, while on a platform in the centre of the room a tumbler who seemed to have no bones in his body tied himself into intricate knots and straightened himself out again.

Haman returned, out of breath and took his place behind the King. In his face an expression of sneering amusement warred with the grave subservience which was its public wear. After a moment Artaxerxes beckoned him again and whispered. "Did you remember to say the royal crown?" That was of importance, for Artaxerxes, whom Vashti accused of colour blindness, had had that crown specially made of sapphires and emeralds set in a network of small diamonds because the blue-green blaze of the stones matched and enhanced the colour of her eyes.

"I remembered, my Lord," said Haman, and stepped back. It was within his power at that moment to add a whispered warning which might have spared his master an imminent humiliation; but in Haman's view it was no part of a serving man's duty to make comments or issue warnings unless they were manifestly to his own advantage. He filled Artaxerxes' goblet and stepped into the background again.

The harpists were replaced by cymbalists and the tumbler retired, the platform was again occupied by the Indian girls who, warming to their subject, danced with even more vigour and abandon. Ten, fifteen minutes passed. Then, at the doorway, there was a slight commotion. The seven dignified chamberlains could be seen . . . and they were behaving rather like seven small boys called for some offence into the presence of their schoolmaster — each was trying to push the other forward and to be last himself. Finally, Zethar, the eldest, a venerable figure with his long white beard, accepted the inevitable, and, followed by all eyes, walked the length of the pavilion and stood before his master.

"My Lord King," he said in a subdued voice, "the Queen refuses to attend you."

Artaxerxes, taking advantage of the improvement of his stomach when his boredom lifted, had been drinking steadily during the last twenty minutes, and was now more than a little drunk.

"Speak up, Zethar," he said loudly, "you mumble like a street beggar."

Zethar, thus admonished, raised his powerful, practised, chamberlain's voice and announced: "My Lord King, the Queen refuses to attend you. She says that it is against the law for women to appear at public feasts."

There was a moment of stunned silence — the stunned silence for which lately the King had wished, and then every man within earshot burst into laughter. This was delectable; far better than any of the staged entertainments. When the King had raised his voice and announced his intentions of clinching the argument about beauty in women by producing a woman of Petra, only one or two who remembered Vashti's origin had imagined that he meant his Queen. And they had been too incredulous to think that he intended to display *her*. The general expectation had centred upon the thought that Artaxerxes had purchased, or been given, some pretty slave girl from Petra; and they had all been prepared to admire her, to agree with their master sycophantically, while preserving their own convictions that Egyptian, Greek, Georgian, Syrian, Phoenician women were actually better looking. Zethar's voice suddenly enlightened them; they laughed with abandonment, both because Artaxerxes had so far forgotten himself as to suggest the Queen's presence at a men's feast, and because apparently there was one living creature who dared defy the man who for the past seven days had been impressing them with his power and omnipotence. Ha, ha, ha!

Artaxerxes mustered his dignity and said: "Very well; we must contrive to manage without her." He was bitterly affronted; and the worst of it was that Vashti was right. The law was on her side; it laid down, quite clearly, the duties and the limitations of women. They were not allowed to appear at public feasts. On the other hand, he — and was he not above the law? — had requested her presence, and she must have known that he had only asked her to appear out of his boundless pride, his love for her. Why must she always shame and reduce him?

He would have sat like a snubbed child, a little sulky, very hurt in his feelings, ready to-morrow to say a few peevish things — and then be taken back into favour.

To-morrow he would have said: "After all, the law is made for common folk, not for kings and queens," and "I only wanted to show them how beautiful you were. Their wives wouldn't tell them for jealousy," and, forced to it, "I was drunk, Vashti, or I wouldn't have suggested such a thing." There was no real malice in his mind as he sat there listening to the laughter; only a fury, passing as a child's disappointment, keen as a child's, and a desire to make it up with her, eager as a child's.

But the laughter had subsided, and amongst Artaxerxes' many and mixed guests two emotions had replaced amusement. A number of them realised that the incident offered them another unexpected chance to flatter him. He was the King of Persia, Ruler of One Hundred and Twenty-seven Provinces — they were his satellites, dependent upon his favour for their very existence. If he were insulted, no matter by whom, it was to their advantage to show their loyal anger. Another group remembered that their own wives were feasting with Vashti; they had heard that saucy answer returned; doubtless they were now laughing even more heartily. The law worked so often to women's detriment, they weren't likely to overlook such a remarkable instance of its being on their side. Every man in the room, who knew in his secret heart that his wife was as able, as witty, as clever as he was himself, and only kept in her humbler place because of the law, had a little misgiving. If the King of Persia allowed his wife to be saucy . . . it boded ill for the peace in many a palace.

The two groups soon found, as groups do, their spokesmen. The leader of the first group was a man named Cashena, who, for two years before, had been an independent Prince. He had resisted the Persians so vigorously, with such genius, that when finally he was overcome by their immensely superior forces, Artaxerxes had honoured, not degraded, him. Cashena, on the night when he had made his submission to Artaxerxes — and been kindly treated, had gone home to his wife, whom he trusted and revered, and said: "I have plied my sword and shed my blood to no avail; now I will ply my tongue and use my wits. The man is an immature ass, more hungry for flattery than your cat is for fish.

Fear nothing, I can re-establish my house upon sweet words." He had then broken his sword across his knee and burst into angry tears. But only his wife knew that. Artaxerxes imagined that he had harnessed Cashena's vigour and genius to the Persian chariot and withal gained a loyal and entertaining friend.

He listened to Cashena now, as in well-balanced sentences the Prince said what a shameful thing it was that in any place and any circumstances the King of Persia should be defied. The law, he said, was administered for the control of the ordinary people; to mention it as a reason for not obeying the King, who was above all laws save his own, was insult, blasphemy.

The second group found its spokesman in a very different sort of man; a minor noble who had been made governor of a province because he was a skilful accountant and a genius at extracting revenue. He was a small man, afflicted by a calamitous stammer; but despite these disadvantages many very well-born women had been willing to marry him because his future, his niche in the great empire, was assured. And he was rich and in good favour with Artaxerxes. However, he had chosen to marry a poor, humble girl, daughter of a Babylonian silversmith, because he had imagined that she would be overwhelmed by his riches and the honour he had done her. Once she was married the girl had proved herself to be a virago with a coarse, most withering sense of humour. Once, when he had been rebuking her for the grossest extravagance, and he had been stammering worse than usual from excitement, she had said: "Look, get one of your clerks to write me an official letter about it, will you? I have an appointment with my hairdresser to-day." And another time when, moved by fury, he had been misguided enough to try to smack her face, she had reached out the large capable hands she had inherited from the silversmith and taken his and just held them, laughing at his impotence. He feared her greatly, and would have divorced her but that all his acquaintances would have laughed and said, "Serves you right for marrying a common Babylonian."

She was feasting in the Queen's apartments at this moment. If Vashti were not punished, sharply, immediately and dramatically punished, his life would be intolerable. Flown now with wine and activated by great fear, he did what he would never ordinarily have dared to do and made a bid for Artaxerxes' attention. Stammering dementedly, he begged the King to punish his wife lest the wives of all true men copied her unseemly defiance of their lords.

Once the two men had spoken, voicing the two separate views, other men were not lacking to come forward and support them and Artaxerxes, in whom the bilious feeling had reasserted itself, who was drunk and angry and overtired like a child that had stayed up too late, was surrounded by faces in which eyes gleamed greasy with flattery or bright with malice, and mouths kept opening and shutting, urging him to action of some sort.

And there was no one there to speak a cool, sensible word for Vashti, for the Princess from Petra had never chosen to make herself popular. She could look at

Artaxerxes and make him feel an upstart, and that same look turned upon the nobles and officials of the Court had an even more devastating effect.

Nevertheless, in all the tumult Artaxerxes might not have committed himself had not Haman have chosen that moment to draw back one section of the curtaining and let the cool night air into the heated pavilion. The boy had been warned that when the guests' faces shone with sweat he was to admit some air; and in the excitement all faces had started to shine; and Haman, ever watchful, moved to the part of the wall where the curtain was hung loose over an aperture; and it happened that the curtain was one of those Tyrian purple ones which had drawn Vashti's criticism. All at once something burst in Artaxerxes' brain; she despised him, did she, called him colour blind, dismissed his most gorgeous arrangements as an exhibition of bad taste. And when he spoke he was avenging not the refusal to obey him, which in his heart of hearts he knew, even then, was justified, but the mounting toll of little insults, little coldnesses, little lacks of appreciation which made up the story of his married life. He said, with a deliberately casual air — as though the behaviour of his Queen was a thing of small importance: "Have no fear, gentlemen. A wife who is not obedient in small matters as well as great, is no wife at all. Henceforth I disown her. And now let us dismiss this trivial matter and return to our pleasure."

The court scribe, whose important and sometimes tedious duty it was to set down all the King's decrees upon the tablets, scuttled away to busy himself with his wax and his stylo. "Queen Vashti is divorced," he wrote.

CHAPTER
THREE

In the morning every road leading from Shushan was busy and colourful with the departing guests. In curtained litters borne by slaves, on the backs of sumptuously trapped mules, or high atop the swaying camels, all the most important ladies of Persia began to travel back to their homes. And everyone was in a chastened mood. Those who were by nature meek were now servile, those who had been proud and dominant were unwontedly pleasant and civil. The events of last night had been quite shattering. They remembered the envy they had felt as Vashti, cool and scornful, had moved amongst them, not bothering to display her treasures, but letting them be seen. They remembered the little incident of the Royal Crown: a stout old Arabian ex-Queen, eager to show that she herself was no upstart, had remarked: "Madam, I thought the Royal Crown of Persia was made of rubies; I remember your predecessor wearing it at my daughter's wedding." And Vashti had smiled her cool little smile and said carelessly: "I believe that was so. But Artaxerxes said rubies were not my stone. He had this one specially made for me. Secretly, I regret to say, for it is far too heavy. If he had consulted me I would have designed something more wearable." And with that she had taken it off and laid it aside as though it were a hair-ribbon. Every woman in the great room had gasped at that — to be the subject of so much adoration, and to care so little about it! Amazement and envy had grown throughout the course of the seven days' visit, and the climax had come when the Queen had returned that insolent answer to her husband. There had been, after that, half an hour, during which even the meekest of wives wondered whether she hadn't been too subservient; while the insolent ones planned fresh indulgences for themselves. And then had come the anticlimax. Somewhere out of sight a man had uttered a sentence and the most beautiful, the most fortunate, the most enviable woman in the world was brought to nothing. The weight of that lovely, specially-designed crown would never bother her again! Even the stammerer's bullying wife could read the lesson in that; and when her husband rode up to the side of her litter to inquire whether she would like to eat her picnic meal now or wait until they had crossed the river, she said: "As you wish, my husband."

Threading their way rapidly through the crowds were the couriers on fresh, unloaded horses, carrying their decree to the uttermost parts of the empire, so that all his subjects, great and small, might know of his divorce. The news would arrive in the distant places to which the guests were returning long before they reached home; and how agog everyone would be to hear the intimate details of the story. Women, already the envy of their fellows on account of their invitation to Shushan, would now gain an added importance, be asked to tell again and again the story of that dramatic evening.

The courier whose despatch was destined for Petra soon outdistanced the guests who were going that way, and eventually overtook and passed a woman, a shapeless huddle of shabby clothing, riding a mouse-coloured mule, which, a keener observer might have noted, was fatter and shinier than the average old countrywoman's mount. The courier, spurring on to the first stopping place where he would obtain refreshment, a fresh horse, and the esteem that comes from being the first to hint at a titillating scandal, took no notice of the woman. Why should he? How should he guess that he carried her name on the tablet in his satchel? How should he know that up to the last evening that woman had been his Queen? He rode on; and from within the dark shadow of the earth-coloured veil that hid her face, the woman's green-blue eyes followed his progress for a moment, with an expression of cool amusement. There he goes, she thought, carrying news of my freedom.

For Vashti was riding back to Petra; to the half-ruined, poverty-stricken rose-red palace where she was born. She was going back to the wild, fierce, cold-hearted, scornful people whom she understood and respected. They would understand and respect her, too; they would know why she returned, bringing with her no shred of what was Artaxerxes'; why she had begged these clothes which even her maid had discarded, and come back on this mule because it was the one which had carried her meagre belongings when she went to her wedding. She was coming home in rather worse case than she had left; for her father had made some effort to fit her out like a Princess — but all those clothes had been given away long ago. But no one would mind, and if her father mentioned the matter she would say: "What are you grumbling about? I brought back the mule, didn't I?" and he would roar with laughter for his sense of humour was exactly her own, and he would see the joke of having been Queen of Persia and having gained precisely nothing, but of having salvaged one's own baggage mule. Oh, she thought, I can hardly bear to wait, to get back to them all again.

Artaxerxes slept late and heavily and woke with an aching head and an immediate, depressing sense of disaster. It took him a moment or two to collect his thoughts and remember the events of the previous evening. As soon as he did so he leapt from his bed, sent chamberlains and slaves scurrying hither and thither, seeking this official and that. The decree must be annulled, he cried; he had never meant to utter it; he had been drunk, over-persuaded, out of his mind. Such an absurdity must never go down on the tablets.

Even while they were telling him that the chief scribe and ten minor ones had sat up all night making copies of the decree, and that the horsemen were already speeding along all the roads in Persia, Artaxerxes was laving his heavy eyes with ice-cold water fresh drawn from a deep well; shaving his cheeks, oiling his beard — too impatient to wait for the ritual attendance of his servants. Hastily and unaided, arguing with Zethar all the time: "If one of my decrees can become an unalterable law, then when I cancel it that can become law too," he struggled into a robe, taking care to choose one which became him, and then, after a glance into the brightly polished sheet of silver that served him for a mirror, he said, "Wait here, all of you. I go to the Queen."

If she understood that he had been drunk when he issued that decree she would forgive him. She was very tolerant of drunkenness; for up in ruined Petra, she had told him, when a dry summer had spoiled the vine harvest and made wine scarce and dear, they had brewed a corn spirit, very harsh to the palate, but potent. And sometimes, when she had been in a mood to entertain him she had told him very amusing stories of her father and brothers and cousins becoming drunk on this brew and performing the most extravagant feats, saying the most unwarrantable things. He would utterly humble himself before her and say that he had been insanely drunk ever to have requested her presence; he would congratulate her upon her good sense in disobeying him, and he would beg her to forgive him. Because without her life was empty and meaningless.

Vashti's apartments were deserted. The great room which she had so cleverly contrived for the entertainment of her guests was littered and disordered, wearing that peculiar air of desolation which comes upon a place where many people have been and which has then been abandoned. The inner apartments were tidier, but equally desolate. There was her silver bed with its turquoise-fringed curtains, and thrown across it was a rose-red robe, with a wilting flower still pinned to the fold of its shoulder. Nearby the Royal Crown lay on its side like a hoop which a child had in boredom abandoned. A pair of sandals, rose-red like the gown, lay on their sides on the white wolfskin rug beside the bed. Her table, with the silver mirror which matched his own, stood by the window space that overlooked the garden, it glittered with rare gems; rings for the fingers, rings for the ears, rings for the ankles, and rings for the toes. Near the head of the bed stood a seven-branched candlestick, and on the table beside it lay a neatly rolled scroll — her bedside reading, with the wooden peg marking her place. "The Rise and Fall of Petra," he read without any sense of jealousy. The whole room spoke her name; it breathed her perfume at him. But there was no sign of Vashti herself.

Shaken by a fear, a premonition which he would not yet acknowledge, he stood in the centre of the room and clapped his hands loudly. Nothing happened, and presently he clapped his hands again. This time, somewhere there was a sound of movement, and after a moment or two a frightened female slave sidled into the room and bowed.

"Where is your mistress?" Artaxerxes demanded.

"The late Queen, my Lord?"

"The Queen," he said furiously. "Why do you speak of her as though she were dead? Where is she?"

"I do not know, my Lord."

He leaned down and shook the already shaking shoulder.

"Tell me then what you *do* know."

The slave raised a terrified face. "My Lord . . . last night, after your decree was known — the . . . the . . . oh, my Lord, what can I call her who knew your favour and then lost it . . . *she* came to this room and sent all away — even the well-born who attended her. Only me, my Lord, she retained, and of me she asked the gift of some old clothes which I did not value, and which could not be priced even in the old clothes market. I brought her what I had, my Lord, for she, in her time, had been good to me. Do not, I pray you, hold that against me; I could not do otherwise. And this morning, very early, she left, my Lord."

"In old clothes," Artaxerxes said, with a glance at the rose-coloured robe on the bed.

"In old clothes," said the slave, "without escort, and riding a baggage mule."

"In what direction?"

"That, my Lord, nobody knows. I did ask. Forgive me that, my Lord King — the taking of interest in one who has fallen from your favour — but to me she was a kind mistress. I did ask, but there was so much commotion this morning; everyone was too busy . . . and nobody cared."

Artaxerxes looked at the cringing slave and thought — no, nobody cares, save only you who remember a kind mistress and I who remember an unkind wife. Unkind, but beautiful and fascinating and very dear.

"Presently," he said, "I will set a scribe to write you out a tablet of manumission. You shall be free from henceforward and draw an annual pension of two gold pieces."

The woman fell to her knees and laid her grizzled head against his feet, too overcome to speak.

"Meanwhile," he said, "straighten these rooms and set all things in order."

For, of course, he thought, hastening back to his own part of the palace, he would get her back. A mule would be easily overtaken. A whole fleet of swift horsemen should set out, carrying news of the rescinding of the decree and searching for Vashti.

But the chamberlains and councillors were of another mind. The immutability of the laws of the Medes and Persians — was it not a byword throughout all the known world? If the great King issued one decree in the evening and cancelled it in the morning, all authority would be set at nought. Why, next time a new order for taxes, or for conscription for the army, was announced men would hesitate and say, "Wait awhile, our King is wont to change his mind overnight as in the case of Vashti." They argued their case cleverly; but it remained for old Zethar, still smarting under Vashti's scornful treatment of him last evening, to speak the convincing word.

"My Lord," he said, "I dare to take the risk of offending you and losing my office and even my head. But I am an old man and my years have brought me wisdom. If you seek out this woman you will put your neck in a yoke compared with which the lowest slave's is a piece of thread. Even the manner of her departure was an insult to you, both as a monarch and man. Shall the King of Persia, master of one hundred and twenty-seven provinces, the ruler whose empire stretches from India to Ethiopia, go sniffing on the trail of a petticoat as a hound sniffs the track of a gazelle? She was a woman of most high stomach, proud manner and evil pride, and if you pursue her now you pay her for her faults; the high stomach, the pride and the insolence will increase tenfold, and you — and all Persia — will suffer for it. Thus and thus I did and was rewarded, she will say, and thus and thus can I do and still be tolerated. My Lord, if you would be master in your own house, much less in your own kingdom, you will let her go and forget her."

It was all true, most dismally true. "Even the manner of her departure . . ." Artaxerxes reflected. Not a word of farewell; just the scornful abandonment of everything that he had given her. The crown tossed aside — the royal crown that he had specially made for her. "What is a crown to me?" Insolence past understanding, arrogance past forgiving.

"I will let her go," he said at last. "And I will forget her. And now, Harbonah, let us have the latest news from Tyre. Have the shipwrights and the sailmakers settled their dispute and is the work going forward?"

The council turned with relief to other business, and one by one the courtiers delivered their decrees; and the mouse-coloured mule growing less sleek and less shiny and more weary pushed on towards Petra, where it arrived in such sorry state that when Vashti actually spoke her words, "I brought back the mule, didn't I?" her father was able to stab through his laughter with the

34

words, "Ah, but I sent him out on four legs and you brought him back on three," which remark caused great hilarity. And Artaxerxes settled himself to his forgetting.

CHAPTER
FOUR

The trouble was that it wasn't easy to forget. And the King of Persia was once more sharing a state of mind with Bisha, the tousled old female slave whom he had freed. She had a little house now, on the outskirts of Shushan, and there was a peach tree in the garden and a plot of artichokes, a prolific vine and some flax. She was busy all day — and so was Artaxerxes occupied with many things; but she missed her mistress, and so did Artaxerxes. Nobody to consider, nobody to please, nobody on whose smile happiness depended. Life was very empty for both of them. Bisha, of course, was envied by everybody in her own class; Artaxerxes was envied by everybody in the world. Bisha's misery meant nothing; Artaxerxes' could cast a gloom over the whole court, over the whole empire. But they were alike in that they both had natures which craved domination and were lost without it.

Nobody realised that Bisha was miserable, so no steps were taken to relieve her misery. Artaxerxes' lack of interest in life and flagging spirits affected everyone who came into contact with him. A crazy tribesman from Kurdistan made a raid across the Indus and Artaxerxes said, "Well, what of it? That territory was never anything but a nuisance," and could not be forced into a campaign of retaliation. A sailor, back from a trip from Cyprus, came into Shushan to pay a visit to his mother who was a cook in the royal kitchen, and fell ill of a new plague. Twenty-three slaves and fifteen persons of other ranks were affected and there was a great panic. Everybody of consequence fled from the city, but Artaxerxes, urged to leave, said, "Where the gods strike, they strike; can it matter whether I be there or here?" And that kept the officials, terror-maddened but impotent, at their posts.

An emperor who cared nothing for his empire nor his personal safety was a source of danger to all sensible men, and very soon the great men of Persia, the sensible men, were putting their heads together and making plans.

Old Zethar, to whom the years had given wisdom, actually voiced the plan which was finally carried forward. To a crony or two he spoke with the utmost frankness, but to Artaxerxes himself he made a more subtle approach.

"My Lord," he said one day with apparent casualness, "those who love you and Persia are a little concerned because of the succession. This recent outbreak of plague has shown us that men can die in their prime. And there are, moreover, the chances of war. We should be happy to see the heir of the throne. The gods grant that your life be long in the land — but when you are gathered to your fathers it would be an ill thing if some decadent Babylonian princeling should inherit . . . Every one of your loyal subjects speaks with my voice, my Lord, when I venture to say that you should take another wife."

"I would gladly oblige you," Artaxerxes said sourly, "and I am not deaf to the soundness of your argument. But I have to live with the woman. There was that Egyptian Princess — her face was too much like one of their Pyramids, wide at the jaw and going up to a point; and the daughter of Palmyra whom you, Zethar, so cunningly brought to Court last month, was so stupid, beautiful but stupid, that ten minutes of her company sent me to sleep. Women aren't what they were, my friend, when you were young."

"My Lord," said Zethar, remembering his talk with his cronies, "you are the greatest, the most powerful King on the face of the earth. There is no need for you to many a Princess or a woman of noble blood. The touch of your hand could ennoble the most lowly. Your empire is wide; surely within its bounds there lives some woman, lovely to look at, intelligent of mind and pleasant of spirit, in whom your majesty might take some pleasure. Could we not seek her out?"

"You and Harbonah, with Bigtha perhaps to give the casting vote," Artaxerxes said. "There are matters, Zethar, which I gladly leave to you, duties I am bound to relegate — but the gods preserve me from a wife of your choosing."

"The gods so preserve you, my Lord," Zethar said patiently. "Our suggestion was far from that. We proposed, with your permission, to send out an order that all the most beautiful young virgins in each of your many provinces should come to Shushan — regardless of their class and upbringing. Those who needed some education could be given it . . . we had regard to the diversity of language and manners in an empire of this size, my Lord. Then, as each one was ready for inspection, we thought that if you invited her to supper and talked for an hour or so. There is a chance," he said, rather humbly, "that one might find favour in your eyes."

Artaxerxes had a flashing, disconcerting vision of a long parade of young creatures, all doing their best, all wearing their finest clothes, trying their little tricks, exhibiting their personalities, trying to be clever. He gave a great sigh.

"You have a curious facility, Zethar, for picking your course and then giving it an irresistible label. 'Ensuring the succession,' you label this, when really you mean merely to make me more cheerful. Very well, have your way. I tell you frankly," he leaned forward and his voice took on an edge, "if you can rake through my provinces and find me one single female who can, for an hour, distract my mind and not set me comparing her unfavourably with Queen Vashti, I will marry her."

Zethar, to whom the years had brought wisdom, ignored this reference to the banished Queen. He pretended that Artaxerxes had given him an order, not accepted a suggestion.

"It shall be done, my Lord. The loveliest young virgins from every province to be sent for your inspection and approval. If I may say so, my Lord . . . such an order will have a beneficial effect from frontier to frontier; be the means of uniting all classes and all nationalities. It is the most truly . . ." he fumbled for a word and, failing to find it, coined a new one, "democratic decree ever issued by a monarch."

"You see to it," said Artaxerxes, very bored.

Zethar, thus given permission, lost no time in having Artaxerxes' half-hearted consent made into a decree; and once more the swift couriers spurred away to the cities and towns and villages which were the outlying centres of the government. The news they carried this time was even more exciting and dramatic than the news of Vashti's banishment. Every girl of marriageable age who was not positively deformed or aggressively ugly, became the centre of her family's attention and hopes. In Babylon and Nineveh, in Palmyra and Petra and Memphis, in sacked Samaria and in royal Shushan alike, the possibility of an impossible day-dream coming true began to beat like a great pulse in the minds of the young girls and in the minds of their guardians. Even far away in the desert places nomad families who chanced to hear the news from some passing caravan, would take muster of their daughters and wonder if the upstanding, sunburnt young shepherdesses might not compare favourably with the pallid products of palaces. Zethar had said that this decree would be a means of uniting the empire, and so far as hope and excitement were concerned, he was a true prophet. Great kings reduced by the force of Artaxerxes' army, petty officials who by their own merits could never rise far, looked to their pretty daughters to accomplish the miracle of reinstatement or advancement. The Royal Queen's crown of Persia lay there, unclaimed, waiting for any girl, *any* girl who could qualify to wear it. Such a chance, such a revolutionary idea, had never been known before on the earth. And men who had no marriageable daughter comforted themselves by taking a wider view. "So great is our King, so mighty that he has no need to make an alliance with any other King by seeking his wife in high places. So royal and so noble is Artaxerxes that he may wed a kitchen slut if so be she takes his fancy. Never before has any monarch been so great and mighty, so royal and noble, as Artaxerxes." The women, especially those who had recently been married, or had lately married away their daughters, were beyond all consolation; if only they had known; if only they had waited.

Zethar, wily old man that he was, had anticipated the excitement and allowed for the triumph of hope over common sense, and so arranged it that before any girl travelled to Shushan at the government's expense she was tested and judged to be marriageable and above the average in beauty. And the tragedies began when certain applicants in every centre of local government failed this first test and were returned to their families as unworthy. They were not to blame that their noses were too large, their eyes too small; and Artaxerxes, himself not an unmerciful man, would have been grieved to think of the heartbreak which his decree had caused. And for the other tragedies too — the shepherdess from the plains of Zabain who passed the first test and then, simple-mindedly seeing herself as the one finally chosen and desperate at the thought of giving up the shepherd boy to whom she had plighted her troth, threw herself down a well; the satrap's daughter, a beautiful little thing who on the morning of her first test was stung by a wasp and arrived with a lopsided face and, despite all her explanations, was sent home, and unable to bear her family's obvious disappointment and the thought of her own ill luck, drank henbane and died in agony. And, less dramatic, there were the girls who were frightened at the thought of marrying a man they had never seen; girls honest enough to know that they would never make adequate queens; a few girls to whom the whole thought of marriage was repugnant; many girls who were already a little in love.

There was plenty of wholehearted co-operation with the scheme, and no little opposition, too. But nowhere in all the one hundred and twenty-seven provinces was there opposition so cool and reasonable as in the house of Mordecai in the Jewish quarter of Shushan.

CHAPTER
FIVE

In this small and humble house, overgrown and yet in a measure supported by the ancient vine which covered it, lived the old Jew whom Artaxerxes had casually mentioned to Vashti — he who had burst into tears and rent his clothes at the sight of Jehovah's sacred vessels being used as kitchenware. With him lived his young niece, Esther, an orphan whom he had brought up to the age of fifteen years. They were very happy together because they were very much alike. Their neighbours regarded them as oddities. Mordecai was a scholar; in the old days, in their own city of Jerusalem, he would have been honoured and revered, lifted high above the common rut of men; even here, in this place where the Jews were merely people conquered by the people whom the Persians in turn had conquered, he could have made a comfortable place for himself had he been so minded. A good number of the cleverer Jews had succeeded in finding places for themselves as scribes, or accountants or stewards. Mordecai took no trouble at all; unlike most scholars, he was clever with his hands and did not despise manual labour. He would work as carpenter, bricklayer, potter, or cobbler, doing whatever job offered itself. He would write or read letters for the illiterate, taking payment, generally in kind, if he thought his client could afford it. He would work out, with great diligence, the family tree of any Jew who feared that, in the captivity, his pedigree might be lost and his chance of forefathering the promised Messiah be obscured; he would explain any point of law or correct procedure to those who were in danger of forgetting. He was, naturally, very poor. Occasionally, when jobs were scarce and hunger threatened the household, Esther, who shared his manual ability, would engage herself to some wealthy household as sempstress or embroiderer, or in a humbler sphere, do the baking, housekeeping, baby-tending for a woman temporarily indisposed. They kept themselves alive and that was all, but in all Shushan there was no couple less concerned with material well-being than Mordecai and Esther; and when, as sometimes happened, there was food in the house for two days ahead they would both settle down happily to read and study and feel themselves completely independent of the world. Motherly women had, at various times during the last year, ventured to remind Mordecai that he had a duty to the girl — she should soon be betrothed to some orthodox Jew; and it was time, they said, tactfully, that she had some other clothes than the simple, much mended, snuff-coloured garment which she wore in cold weather, or the equally old white linen robe which was her summer wear. They said that she would ruin her eyes and round her shoulders with reading. Mordecai, who had great innocence in worldly matters, was a little troubled by these admonitions and sometimes felt guilty because he had reared this girl, Esther, exactly as he would have reared a boy. But when he reported such a conversation to Esther she only laughed; and very soon Mordecai forgot so trivial a matter and their happy life continued smoothly. The house was very clean, for Esther had a curious fastidiousness in some matters; but it was very untidy, littered with scrolls and the tools of their various trades and an assortment of treasures which Mordecai, as a trusted man, had taken into his keeping for other Jews who had never succeeded in finding a settled home in Persia, and quite a few heirlooms awaiting the arrival of some known, but unlocated heir, lost in the Dispersion.

To this house Mordecai returned on the midday after Artaxerxes' decree had been posted in the market-place at Shushan. It was a very hot morning, and for a moment after his arrival Esther wondered whether he was suffering from a touch of sunstroke. There was a curious, suppressed excitement about him, and as soon as he entered the shady house he dragged her to the window and said, "Esther, let me look at you." Holding her by the shoulders he stared into her face and then stepped back, considering her as a whole until Esther felt her face redden and her whole pose stiffen into awkwardness. Then he turned away, as though deeply satisfied and dropping down to the bench near the door said, "Esther, I believe we have a chance."

"Of what, Mordecai?"

"Of gaining a powerful representative of our race at Court."

"You?" she asked, delight in her voice. Perhaps his qualities as an historian and scribe had been recognised at last.

"Not I, my dear. You."

That confirmed her worst fears. "You have been smitten by the sun," she said, and hastened away to get a wet rag for his head. She knew how he would stand at any corner to give advice or argue a point.

Mordecai accepted the rag gratefully, though with scorn.

"My head can do with cooling," he admitted, "though it is not the sun that has set it awhirl. It is the notice in the market-place . . ."

"He isn't . . . sending us . . . home?" Esther asked breathlessly voicing the dearest, the foremost hope of every Jew in Persia.

"Not yet. Though even that . . . even that might result."

"Oh, what are you talking about?" she asked impatiently. These broken, hesitating inconclusive sentences were so unlike his usual concise and scholarly way of talking.

Briefly he told her.

"It is the sun — or else you are out of your mind," she said. "I'm pretty enough; but all the loveliest, all the really beautiful women in the empire will be displaying themselves, and how should I compare? Besides, I wouldn't dream of doing anything so silly. He must be crazy to think of such a way of choosing a wife. As bad as a blind auction."

46

"Eliezer sent out to choose a wife for our forefather, Isaac, selected Rebekah by equally blind chance," said Mordecai, solemnly. "One must, you know, my dear, make a *little* allowance for the hand and the will of God."

"Take then the most fantastic view, and imagine that out of all this horde of women I should be the one chosen. How would *that* work in with the will of God? Who would be benefited, except possibly me?"

"Our whole race, my child." The old man brooded deeply for a moment. "*If* you were chosen . . . I am not suggesting that any immediate difference would be felt or seen; influence grows slowly. But the influence which a good, loyal, attractive wife can wield is in the end practically infinite. If you could marry Artaxerxes, Esther, we Jews should always have, in the very heart of Persia, a most powerful ambassador. Not an agent, not an agitator, I am not thinking of that, but a voice to speak the right word at the right time. There are stormy times ahead for us, you know. With every day that passes and that sees us adhering to our own old faith, our own old customs, we grow more unpopular. We are an indigestible people. And that which cannot be absorbed is always hated. The time is coming when a friend at Court will be badly needed."

"And before that time comes," Esther said calmly, "God will provide it without help from me. *He* knows that I have no desire to marry anyone. I want to stay here with you and lead this life which suits us both; and if, when you are gathered to your fathers, the idea of getting married does arise in my mind I shall choose a man of my own race, and of my own kind, a scholarly man. In fact, a man as like you as possible. There, doesn't that flatter you?"

"On the contrary, it distresses me beyond measure. It shows me how right Martha was when she said I was rearing you badly. *You* don't want to get married, *you* want to stay here, *you* will choose when you should marry and whom. Esther, that is no way for a well-bred Jewess to talk."

"I am sorry to have distressed you," Esther said, with conventional politeness. "It may be your fault for having reared me to respect the truth. And I might well retort that you have distressed me too. You speak of us Jews being indigestible — and is it not a fact that that is largely due to our avoidance of mixed marriages. Since our race began Jew has married Jew; and if you are honest you will admit that had any man of another race asked for my hand you would have been the first to object and express repugnance."

"That is true, Esther. But there are times when the law is superseded by the direct will of God. It is against the law to kill one's child yet Abraham was prepared to slay Isaac in obedience to God's command. It is forbidden to sell one's brother into slavery — yet the slavery of Joseph was the means of preserving all our people."

"Doing ill that good may come of it. That is a dangerous doctrine. For the ill can be seen, here and now, the good remains hidden. And how can a simple person distinguish between the ill that is mere ill and the ill which brings forth good?"

48

"There is one safe rule," Mordecai said gravely, "and that is to obey one's elders." That sentence was so unlike him that she looked up quickly to see whether he were really teasing her; but there was no twinkle in his eye at all.

"You mean," she said, slowly, "that it is my duty to obey you in this and enter myself for this undignified ... beauty competition? That is what it is. Vulgar, undignified ... a cock fight."

"Our father Jacob was vulgar and undignified when he cheated Laban over the spotted lambs, Esther; but he thereby laid the foundation of all the herds of Israel. You will excuse me for saying this, I trust, but the minds of women are limited and apt to be over-literal and yours shares the fault of your sex."

"Oh," said Esther and closed her mouth against the sharp retort that arose. In one half hour she had been told, for the first time in her life, that blind obedience to one's elder was a duty; and that women had inferior minds. She went away to think these things over.

It was some little time before the subject was mentioned again. The old happy life flowed on and Esther had begun to hope that Mordecai had either forgotten or changed his mind. And then one evening as they sat at their simple supper of bread, milk, and ripe fruit, Mordecai said abruptly: "Esther, to-morrow is the day when the first tests for this part of the city takes place. I need hardly tell you, need I, that there is nothing further from my thought than the desire to force my will on you. You should know by now that I value your love above all things, and that you are the very heart of my heart and have been since, long ago, you came into my care. I do not wish to force you to enter this contest, or to enter it unwillingly, but I wish most fervently that you would do so, for the sake of your own people, and to please me."

"You make it very difficult for me to refuse without seeming ungrateful, disobedient, disloyal, and churlish," Esther said. "I wish you would answer me one question, honestly."

"I have always endeavoured to answer all your questions — honestly," said Mordecai, remembering some more awkward ones she had asked him in the past.

"If I refused, would you compel me?"

Mordecai stared at her gravely for a moment and then said:

"Yes. With regret, Esther; but in the conviction that I was acting rightly."

"I am glad to know that," she said. "Because that takes the decision out of my hands. If I agree, I go, and if I refuse, I go. Very well, then, I go. And after to-morrow it will be in other hands than yours and mine — the decision, I mean."

"It is always in other hands — God's hands, my dear. To-morrow two of the palace officials appointed to the office will stand in the covered part of the Corn Market which has been transformed, by the way, into a place of palatial splendour — and they will select those virgins they think fit for the King's inspection. But they are only instruments. Jehovah knows at this moment upon whom the final choice will fall."

50

"That, in general, is a profound and very disturbing thought," Esther said. "But at the moment it is comforting. It means that I need do nothing."

"What nonsense," Mordecai said. "The will of God is above us, but it works *through* us. In every trade there are good tools and bad tools; the bad are discarded, the good are cherished. And it lies within our choice to be good tools or bad."

"Then the judges to-morrow will be tools of a sort. How can they be good or bad?"

"By judging fairly or unfairly. Suppose, for the sake of argument, one of them favoured a candidate who was obviously unworthy; he might advance her claims; he would thus be acting against his orders, against his better judgment, against the will of God. He would thus be a bad tool and finally he would be discarded. It is all very simple.

"Then to-morrow I put on my best white robe — having washed myself thoroughly — smooth out what Martha calls my scholar's scowl, and straighten my shoulders and then I shall be a good tool. Is that so?"

"Precisely," Mordecai said, with relief and pleasure in his voice. "And now since you have decided to take this sensible view I will tell you something that I heard to-day in the city. Something that has a connection with the first conversation we ever held on this subject. There is a young man called Haman; he is the son of Hammedatha, an Amalekite — you know what that means for *us* — the bitterest enemy in the world. He entered the King's service as a menial, but he attracted notice and courted favour, and for some little time now has been granted special treatment. Lately a few well-born courtiers ventured to — well, one doesn't *complain* exactly to the Lord of Persia — but they pointed out that the situation was slightly irregular; and yesterday Artaxerxes answered them by making him a noble. He is now Lord of the Eastern Gate, is entitled to wear scarlet and fur, and draws revenue from all the area between the city boundary and the brickyard; and he will go further. He is — naturally, for he was so born — a confirmed Jew-hater, and I tell you frankly, my child, that were it not for the hope and trust which I repose in *you*, I should have the very gloomiest thoughts about our future as a race."

Esther was silent for a moment. Then she leaned across the table and said seriously: "Uncle Mordecai, I do love you and I do respect you, and I am grateful to you for all you have done for me . . . but I must say this. You set too high a value on me. You don't know anything about women; you've never been married; you've never had any dealings with any woman except old Martha and me. You don't *know* how lovely, how dazzlingly beautiful women can be. To-morrow we shall go to the Corn Market and you will see. You'll see women who could murder their mothers and fathers, their husbands and fifteen children — and have the sympathy of every man who looked on them, because of their beauty. I'm saying this because I don't want you to be disappointed to-morrow when I come home, rejected."

"But Esther, you are very beautiful. Lately I have thought that God gave you this beauty that it might be used, now."

"Mordecai, I am not *beautiful*. I am merely pretty. My hair is nice; and I have the eyes you say Hadassah, my grandmother, had, which do make rather a startling contrast to the black hair; but my top lip is too short and my lower one too full, and my nose isn't absolutely straight. But there, you will see to-morrow . . ."

"I shall see," Mordecai said. "So long as you present yourself in good will I am content to leave the rest to God."

"And so am I," said Esther, falling back on the thought that if Jehovah had really intended to make her Queen of Persia, He would have devised some method a little more certain than this. If the test had been one for scholarship she would have been more confident of her chances — and more frightened lest she should pass. As it was, though she dutifully washed and then oiled her long black hair and made a few other innocent little preparations, she faced the morrow's ordeal in a spirit of light-hearted cynicism. There would be so many more beautiful women . . .

CHAPTER
SIX

Mordecai and Esther walked to the Corn Market at ten o'clock the next morning. It was a hot and rather breathless day and Esther let her veil fall loosely. Before they had left the Street of Camels, where their little house stood, they could see, in the bigger street beyond, an unwonted amount of traffic; litters and palanquins, mules, donkeys, and horses and camels were carrying girls and their attendants towards the Corn Market. The air was thick and yellow with stirred-up dust. Mordecai paused in his stride and said:

"I should have thought of that. I should have hired a litter. Go you back, Esther, and wait and I will run and ask Joab for the litter in which his mother-in-law goes to the synagogue. If I carry one end and he the other he can hardly charge me more than three copper pieces."

"You would waste your errand," said Esther. "Miriam, the baker's daughter, bespoke that litter a fortnight ago."

"You should have thought of it yourself," said Mordecai, a little irritably. "You should have known that it was essential to arrive looking fresh and unfatigued." The peevishness in his voice betrayed to Esther the importance he attached to this excursion.

He began to walk on again. "At least," he said, "draw your veil closer . . . Your hair looked so beautiful, it would be a pity if the dust dulled it."

Oh dear, Esther thought, obediently drawing the veil closer, he is going to be so miserable, so disappointed, so downcast, when we walk home again; blame me for not thinking of the litter; blame himself . . ."

They reached the Corn Market where the candidates for the first test were ushered into a great waiting room where there was every convenience for the repair of beauty; scented water in porcelain bowls, soft towels, silver mirrors, brushes, cosmetics, pins. Outside this door Mordecai was halted and bidden wait and Esther, entering the place alone, realised that she was the only girl unaccompanied by a female relative. Many had three. Every woman seemed to be in a frenzy, arranging a gown's fold, pinning in a flower, adjusting a jewel, arranging a curl. "Smile, Nana, do remember to smile, your teeth are your best feature," one woman was whispering, over and over again. "Your gown is creased; I *told* your father to bring Chinese silk. Oh dear, oh dear, the fool said the clothes did not matter. He's ruined us . . ." "Darling, I am not quite sure about that rose . . . it is brighter than your lips, and that is bad. Let me pin it here, lower down. There, now it does not detract . . ."

Gabble, gabble, gabble, Esther thought, waiting her turn at the mirror, and when it came leaning close to see if the dust *had* dulled her hair. It hadn't and, with hands which seemed suddenly cold and clumsy, she threw the veil back into its original position and stood aside. She remembered a sentence in a book by an obscure philosopher called Balas: "The trouble with women is that their minds are so easily distracted from great matters to trivialities. And yet why should I say 'trouble' since this attention to small things does in great measure contribute to man's comfort?" Well, she thought, probably all this attention to detail will, in the end, contribute to Artaxerxes' comfort. But there was no other detail to which she could attend; so she left the place of preparation and went out and stood quietly by Mordecai, who at least did not now admonish or advise her, and waited until her name was called.

The ordeal, when it came, was horribly like being exposed in the Slave Market. (They should have held the contest there, Esther thought, irrelevantly.) Two men, with bored expressions, asked her to open her mouth and studied her teeth; looked at her hands, paying attention to her nails. They came close, as Mordecai had done, and studied her face, and then moved away, as he had done, and looked at her figure. Loathing it all, but patient, she turned this way and that, walked, stood, as they directed, and was finally handed a little red seal of stamped wax attached to a piece of purple ribbon. She said "Thank you," as she said it when Elias the fishmonger handed her the piece of salt fish for which she had bargained and then, dismissed, went through another door and into a corridor, where to her relief she found Mordecai waiting.

"They gave me this," she said, holding out the little seal, unaware of its significance.

"God be praised," said Mordecai. He saw the lack of understanding on her face and added, "It is the sign of the chosen. It means, my dear child, that I must leave you here. You will be taken up to the palace and wait your turn with the other chosen for the King to approve of you."

"Do you mean," Esther asked sharply, "that I cannot come home with you?"

"But of course. You are now one of the selected candidates. They cannot go *home*; for many of them home is a thousand miles away. You and they, will now go up to the palace and there the second test will take place."

He turned towards her suddenly and bent and kissed her on the forehead. "My darling, my dear one, I now hand you over to God's keeping. Be mindful, be diligent. I may not linger now but I will write to you. I will tell you all that is in my heart. But they are waiting. Good-bye. God keep you."

She watched him join the stream of girls who had been rejected and their crestfallen keepers; and as she turned aside to pass through a door which an attendant was holding open she saw that envy shone in the eyes of the girls and of the old women. And her first, most immediate emotion was — I'd change with you. I'd love to be going home to the place I know, to make the supper . . . and go on with to-morrow just like yesterday . . . But hard on the heels of that thought came another — this is the hand of Jehovah. Nothing else could have arranged my being selected; there were a dozen at least better looking than I am. Could

Mordecai be right . . .? She saw a lovely girl, with hair like the sun, show her red seal and come running towards the special door. Vanity, vanity, she thought. By some accident I have passed the first test . . . but the other remains. Still humble and hopeful of eventual freedom, she passed through the doorway and joined the excited dozen girls in the inner room.

CHAPTER
SEVEN

When all the young women who had passed the first test were assembled in the Palace at Shushan, the place resembled an enormous girls' finishing school or the harem of Solomon the Great. There were over five hundred of them, all told, and they came from every corner of the empire. The problems of accommodation and of language loomed large and greatly bothered Hegai, Artaxerxes' chief eunuch, who had been given complete control and responsibility. The question of accommodation he solved by dividing off into compartments the great pavilion where the famous feast had been held, and the old divisions were reared again, and some new ones made in the Queen's apartments. Each of the five hundred women was given some slaves to attend her, and the language problem was solved by the arrival of a crowd of interpreters, who also had to be housed and attended. Long before the end of the first week Hegai was heartily sick of his post, and beginning to wonder whether the reward which Artaxerxes had promised him — seven hundred gold pieces and an estate outside Nineveh — was worth all the exertion and the worry. Every day, it seemed, some new crises arose. There was a young sheep girl from

Esdraelon, for example, who had never before slept under a roof, and who, housed in a small inner chamber with painted walls, went almost mad from claustrophobia and sprang at the walls like a crazed cat, tearing them with her nails and screaming. For her Hegai had to rear a little black tent in the centre of a rose garden. And there was an Egyptian Princess from Thebes who not only refused to share a bathroom with any other woman, but demanded that her exclusive bath should be filled every day with asses' milk. And there was a beautiful red-haired, blue-eyed girl from beyond the Taurus who could not eat anything that Hegai offered. There was no interpreter for her, either. She had been the only candidate to enter for the test at Konia in the North, and had been escorted down to Shushan by three gigantic fellows in fur hats, riding small active ponies with flowing tails. They had delivered her into Hegai's keeping, snatched at the bridle of the pony she had ridden, wheeled round and galloped away. She had the coveted red seal with the purple ribbon, and it was stamped with the Konia mark; so Hegai knew she had qualified and where she came from. But nobody understood a word she said, nor could anybody make her understand; and when Hegai had racked his brains and produced every single thing which counted in Shushan as food, he had to admit himself defeated. It never occurred to him to offer her a handful of dry corn and a cup of mare's milk, for no one had ever told him about the Kurds who lived with, on, and *like* horses; and the girl being unable to explain and cut off from the stables, where in five minutes she could have found the only food she had known since she was weaned, sickened and died. And Hegai, looking at her red hair, felt that he had lost his master a treasure, and that if Artaxerxes came to hear of it his pension might be in danger. And there were many, many other minor troubles too; petty jealousies, quarrels — the Greek girl had brought her own hairdresser with her, so six other women must send home for theirs; the girls from the North suffered from the heat, the girls from the South shivered with cold; many were desperately homesick, and many more desperately greedy, for food, for clothes, for service.

Hegai soon sorted them out into three groups — those he detested, those he tolerated and those he positively liked. And he liked Esther, although he was convinced that she was utterly mad and had been sent here by some glaring mistake on the part of the first judges. At the first formal visit he paid her she had asked him whether the King owned a library, and if so might she read what was in it. So long as she had books and a light to read by, she gave no trouble at all.

Every girl's name had been imprinted upon a little tablet, and all the tablets had been placed in a casket. Each morning a blind slave put his hand into the casket and drew out a tablet, and then the bearer of the name upon the tablet was warned that in the evening she would take supper and spend an hour with the King. Hegai noticed that the blind slave always ran his hand round the casket and chose from the third corner, and each morning Hegai had a struggle with himself to refrain from fixing the tablets. If a woman were troublesome Hegai wanted her to meet the final test and go away ... on the other hand, suppose the troublesome one met with Artaxerxes' approval and remained as Queen. That would be horrible — not for Hegai, who would be far away, safe and free on his estate in Nineveh, but for all the other palace servants; and Hegai, if he had little else, had class loyalty. So he refrained from arranging the tablets. And every morning the blind slave dipped in his hand; and every morning one woman walked across the garden and spent an hour and took a meal with Artaxerxes, and every morning one of Hegai's troublesome charges went home — rejected, disappointed, furious, or hopelessly subdued. Hegai, in his curious detached way, would feel sorry for each one. But after all, there were over five hundred of them, and only one could be Queen of Persia — they must have realised that; and each one would go home, in a way, with the King's seal upon her and should make a good marriage.

When the Greek girl, who had had a very choice apartment, went to her test and was rejected and set out, accompanied by her hairdresser, for her home, Hegai moved Esther into the vacant room. He excused this favouritism by saying sourly: "The light in there will be better for you to read by. It will save a few candles."

There was one thing — besides the lack of trouble she gave and her obvious oddity — which fixed Esther in Hegai's mind. Every morning without fail an old man, very shabby but very clean, came and waited by the doorway of the women's palace. He never did anything to draw attention to himself, he just waited until about an hour before midday when Hegai, who since seven o'clock in the morning had been listening to complaints, settling problems and arranging for the evening visit by the chosen one to the King's apartment, went into the porter's lodge to take his mid-morning refreshment. At that moment, regular as the sun, the clean, shabby old man would step forward and ask, "Is Esther well this morning?" And Hegai would say, "Yes, very well. She is reading . . ." and he would mention the latest scroll taken from the palace library by name. The old man would say, "Good, very good. I am happy to hear that she pursues her studies." Then he would go away. Very occasionally he would say, "Perhaps you will kindly deliver this to her." And this might be anything — a little posy of flowers, a few figs in a basket, a letter, a linen handkerchief, a small cake. Once the bundle was large and Mordecai's expression extremely apologetic:

"I wonder if you would ask her if she would mend this for me. I can do most things but I cannot *darn*; and Martha, who has looked after me lately, has taken to bed with twins. Esther will be glad to hear that — after all this time." Hegai was glad that Esther would be pleased by something — for surely no candidate for queenship would be pleased by the sight of a ragged old kaftan that needed darning. In fact, Hegai, delivering the parcel and the message, felt bound to say, "Why don't you ask me for a new robe for your relative. The orders were that the selected ladies could ask for *anything*, positively anything, they required, and you, so far, have asked for nothing save books."

Esther laughed: "It may come to that, Hegai, if I stay here long enough. I can mend this — and it may last another three months. Shall I be here in another three months' time do you think?"

"Let me see. Oh yes. There were five hundred of you. Nine months and two weeks have now passed — about two hundred and ninety of you have been inspected. Two hundred and ten still to be tested. Oh yes, you might be here in three months' time. And if you are, ask me for a new robe."

"I will," said Esther.

She unfolded Mordecai's ragged old robe and it smelt of him and of the little house and of the Street of Camels. She felt very homesick as she threaded her needle. In times past, forced to perform some task or to go out to some job, she had sometimes thought how lovely it would be to be able to read all day. Now for nine months she had done nothing but read and she was rather bored. Even this darning was a relief. She shook the robe out and saw, pinned inside the sleeve, a small papyrus. She spread it out hastily, realising that Mordecai had something to communicate which he had not wished anyone else to learn. I might have known she thought, that he would not care how ragged he was.

The letter said that the time must now surely be approaching when she must face the final test. He wished her well and would remind her of what he had said about the inadvisability of disclosing her race.

"Every day the feeling against us increases," he wrote. "Craft must be met by craft. If you can, establish yourself and leave the rest to God."

She mended the old robe and sent it back with a message: "I am mindful of all that you bid me." And another fortnight passed and fourteen disappointed women went home. And one morning the blind slave held out a tablet to Hegai, who read, "Esther."

CHAPTER
EIGHT

At sunset Hegai parted the curtains and looked towards the place where Esther was sitting. She was crouched upon one end of the divan and, before her and on the floor around, the scrolls spilled out their lettered folds. She had been holding her head in her hands as she read, and her hair, usually so smooth — the best thing about her, Hegai thought — was roughened and disarranged. And the effort of reading in the rapidly fading light had brought a slight scowl to her forehead. Once again Hegai assured himself that this was a woman utterly and completely crazy. And he thought wryly that a visit from a mad woman would at least be a diversion for the King, who had, in the last year, sampled every possible kind, but not, so far as Hegai could judge, any as demented as this one. Nevertheless, he had had his orders and must obey them. So he said in a voice that gave no clue to his feelings:

"Lady, it is the hour of sunset; shortly the King will expect you. Is there anything you require? May I remind you that anything you desire in the way of raiment or ornament is at your command."

"You may bring me a candle — or better still, a lamp," Esther said, looking up from the scroll and pushing her hair from her brow. Then, narrowing her eyes to look at Hegai, she said with a kindness roughened by impatience: "Why do you *worry* so, Hegai? You worry overmuch. Within five minutes, if you hurry with the light, I shall have refreshed my memory of this story; and within another five I shall be ready to enter the King's presence. And even were I not, you, having reminded me of the time and offered me your assistance, would not be to blame. So why do you worry?"

He wanted to say that he worried because, if she entered the royal presence unsuitably clad and appointed, he might be blamed: he wanted to say that every other candidate for Artaxerxes' favour had spent the whole afternoon and as much of the evening as was allowed her in bathing and dressing and arranging her hair. But such speech would have wasted another moment or two of precious time, and since this woman had asked for nothing but a light to read by, Hegai hastened away and returned with a lamp. Esther said "Thank you," and went on reading as though eternity stretched before her.

At the end of five minutes, however, she reached the end of the scroll, rolled it and the others quickly into shape and turned towards her mirror. With rapid fingers she unpinned and combed her long black hair and coiled it again in the heavy roll at the back of her shapely head. Leaning forward she regarded herself critically in the silvery depths of the polished mirror and frowned. Hastily she smeared the paste of rose petals across her mouth and brushed her flushed cheeks with powder, and then leaned forward again, and then stepped backward, until she could see herself reflected from neck to knees. Ought she to have borrowed a robe from the many which had been put into Hegai's keeping for the use of the visiting virgins. The robes had been provided by Artaxerxes' express order so that no girl, however poor, or from however outlandish a province, need be at a disadvantage. People who liked the man in Artaxerxes, as distinct from the King, saw in such an order the working of a fundamentally fair and just mind; others said that he was so little interested in the girls, so heart-sick for Vashti, that the more the girls were levelled out the better he liked it. Esther had seen the collections of dresses: of Indian muslin, Chinese silk, Tyrian purple stuff, heavy cotton beautifully embroidered by peasants in the wild lands beyond the Taurus mountains, Egyptian linen so fine that a whole gown of it could be held in the hand as easily as a lily stem. She had seen, too, the three caskets of jewels, great rubies as large as peach stones, and redder than sunset, emeralds like the grass on Lebanon in springtime, milky opals and moonstones, hyacinth-blue sapphires, lustrous pearls dredged up from the Gulf. She remembered them now, not without a certain longing. But she was too proud to desire to appear in the King's presence wearing borrowed clothes and finery. She would go in the garb and the ornaments which were her own and which were, from long use, almost as much part of her as her own skin — the clean white linen which had been woven in her grandmother's house in far-away

Bethlehem-Judah; the heavy silver necklet, earrings and bangles studded with turquoise which her other grandmother had been wearing on the morning when Nebuchadnezzar's men marched into Jerusalem, and which the old woman, on her deathbed, had bequeathed to Mordecai's daughters when they were begotten. Mordecai had had no daughters and, on the morning of Esther's fourteenth birthday, he had taken the little treasures out of the chest and blessed them and given them to her with a pious word or two of admonition that she must always behave in a manner worthy of such inheritance. Esther had been bored and embarrassed at the time, as she often had been in her early years by her uncle's little sermons; but to-night, in a strange palace with an awful ordeal before her, she found herself strengthened and encouraged by her possession of the small heirlooms and by the memory of Mordecai's words.

Hegai, with some little black torch-bearers in attendance, parted the curtains again and said, "The time is now." Esther turned from the glass and, with a final glance at the scrolls, breathed an inward prayer couched in conventional Hebrew terms: "And now, Lord God of Israel, Isaac and of Jacob, strengthen me, Thy servant, for this task." And to Hegai she said, "I am ready." Hegai thought that truly the very mad were easy to deal with. This one had asked for nothing save a candle, was ready when bidden, and did not embarrass or bother him by asking whether she looked nice and whether there was anything to be frightened of. After a year of daily dealings with the candidates for

Queenship, Hegai was extremely bored with women — women, that is, sane enough to realise how much was at stake and just mad enough to imagine that the crown of Persia was theirs for the taking. This really mad woman with her scrolls and her candles had been a pleasant change. He imagined that later to-night, after she had been dismissed from the King's apartments, he would be sent for and reprimanded about her appearance. But he had done what he could and had witnesses to prove it. He would say to Artaxerxes, "That one was mad, my Lord," and by that time, of course, the King would have realised that for himself.

The procession set out across the garden. Two little torch-bearers walked first, then Hegai, ponderously, dignified, then Esther, flanked on either side by torches, and then a final couple who, out of sight and — they judged — of hearing by Hegai, jigged and skipped and pinched one another so that the light from their torches jumped up and down until Esther turned round and said in a small, mild and yet somehow commanding, voice: "Don't do that. You make me think that you have set my gown afire."

"And a pity that would be," murmured the more obstreperous little black boy; but thereafter he and his companion walked sedately.

And so they reached the door of Artaxerxes' most private apartment, the place wherein he ceased to be King of Persia. Lord of Many Lands, Great Ruler of One Hundred and Twenty-seven Provinces, and became just a man with feet which ached and must be comforted in slippers, flesh which became dirty and

70

must be bathed, a stomach which must be filled and a mind which must be entertained or die of boredom.

The door was of beaten copper inlaid with silver and ivory. Hegai touched some secret spring and it opened, silently swinging upon well-oiled hinges. As it opened he and the torch-bearers stepped aside and Esther, drawing a long deep breath, moved forward alone. Behind her the door swung and closed.

She found herself standing at the top of a flight of six marble steps, down the centre of which a strip of rose-coloured carpet ran. At either end of each step there stood a marble vase out of which flowers and ferns brimmed so that it was like walking through a garden. The room to which the six steps led was small, octagonal in shape, and walled in silk. In its centre stood a long, low table, decorated with flowers and set with vessels of gold, and upon its further side was a couch of gold with cushions that matched the walls.

At one end of the couch a man was sitting; and he sat still until she had descended the six steps and then rose and came to meet her, stretching out one hand, into which she put her own.

"You are welcome," he said pleasantly. "Your name, I know, is Esther, and for this evening we will dispense with all ceremony and you will kindly call me Artaxerxes, without title or formality."

"A name thus ordered into use, my Lord, becomes a title in itself," Esther said, smiling, "so if I forget and call you Lord or Majesty by mistake, I beg you to forgive me."

It occurred to him that every other woman, bidden to call him by his personal name, had immediately taken advantage of it and incorporated it into her first sentence of greeting. But without saying anything of this he led her by the hand and seated her upon the golden couch. And then, as was his custom, because he had found that such a remark put even the most terrified girl at ease, he said, "You are very beautiful."

Esther said gravely, "An expert's opinion upon any subject is always valuable." She waited until Artaxerxes, after a brief moment of doubt, smiled; then she smiled too and added, "Wouldn't you admit that that, or any other sentence, would gain in point if one could add 'my Lord'?"

Artaxerxes thought that over for a moment and said: "I believe it would. Maybe that was why titles were invented, to lend point to the remarks of courtiers." He grinned, and for a second his face bore a great resemblance to that of a naughty boy. "By the Light of the Sun," he said, "most of their remarks need a little help. Wouldn't you agree, Esther?"

"I am without experience of courtiers' conversation. Is it duller than that of women? Clothes, cosmetics, the meaning of dreams, food, little ailments and then clothes and cosmetics again. Not," she added, with a little bitterness in her voice, "that we are to blame for that. One speaks of what one knows, and women are only supposed to know about clothes, cosmetics, dreams, food and little ailments."

Artaxerxes laughed and reached for the slim-necked golden wine flask. Pouring the wine he said:

72

"That sounds as dull as the courtiers' chatter, to be sure. But why do you notice it, Esther? I notice the courtiers' because I am not a courtier — but you *are* a woman."

"A man reared me," Esther said. Her voice took on a note of reminiscence so fond that it was almost homesick. "He wasn't my father — I am an orphan — but this man took me into his house and treated me as though I were his daughter. No . . . " — she corrected herself hastily — "as though I were his son. Only during the past year have I known how much I owe him. There have been times when I have been ungrateful, resentful, almost hating him. When I was small, for example, and had no toys and was not allowed to play with the other little girls, and must stay indoors and learn to read and study the books that seemed so very dull to me then. How I used to wish that I had been brought up by anyone else. But lately I have been so grateful . . . so *very* grateful."

"Any why lately? Why in the past year?"

"I have been a prisoner for a year, Artaxerxes."

"Come, come," he said with humorous testiness. "That is strange talk. Or tell me," his face took on sternness, "have you any complaints? Were you not well treated? Was not everything done for your comfort? Be honest, be frank."

"Everything was done for my comfort. I have in the past year enjoyed more luxury than I ever dreamed of. But one who is not free to come and go, one who is told 'You may walk here and not there,' is a prisoner, Artaxerxes, however well fed and housed. That is why I am so grateful to the man who reared me. Thanks to him I have been able to wander in Egypt and Palestine and Arabia at will. At least . . ." she smiled, "that was in a great measure thanks to you also."

"How?"

"You gave orders that your guests might demand anything in reason, and when I asked for books Hegai brought them, and when I asked for candles he brought them, too. So I come to you this evening, Artaxerxes, not, as you may think, from across the garden from the women's quarters but straight from Phoenicia. You can almost smell the salt sea wind in my hair."

"So that is what it is," he said, taking up her fancy. "I knew it was something strange and rare. At least I knew that you didn't smell of musk, Esther. No, seriously, I did notice that. I am very tired of the scent of musk and of spikenard and of cassia. I like the scent of the sea wind of Phoenicia. It was the home of my ancestors, you know."

Esther thought of the dry, acrid, bracing scent of the cedars of Lebanon which had brushed the nostrils of her ancestors. She said: "If I were a Phoenician I should wish . . . in fact I think I should try to pretend that I belonged to one particular family. I don't suppose, my Lord, that you have ever heard of them? They were poor and they were obscure, but they performed feats of seamanship which have never been equalled in the history of the earth and, one day, when Ethelbaal and all his tribe are forgotten, I think that people, looking backward, will hail them with honour and astonishment. I was reading about them this afternoon."

74

"And their name?" Artaxerxes asked.

"Silashi," Esther said, "the Silashi of Tyre. One of them owned the ship that sailed to the southernmost point of the earth. It took three years, and the ship was small, too small to carry all the stores for that length of time. But he was a man. He carried sacks of corn with him, and when he saw a suitable place on the coast of the continent he skirted he planted the seed and waited and reaped the harvest, and then went on again. That meant immediate self-denial, and there were times when his crew, who did not completely share his dream of voyaging farther than anyone else had ever voyaged, said: 'Let us eat this corn and turn back.' But he would not. He planted his corn and went hungry, he reaped his harvest and went on. He reached the point where the dry land ceases. But that was not all. His son was a weakling who lived and died in Tyre with nothing to his credit but the fact that he remembered until his old age the stories which his father had told him in his childhood. He told them to his son and fired *him* with ambition. That boy, grandson of the other, worked in the dye works for twenty years and saved his money until, at the age of forty, he had enough to buy a ship. He then worked another five years until he had the money to hire the crew and victual it, and then he set out. *He* reached an island in the west. A wild, uncivilised place where men went naked and painted themselves blue in order to make themselves look terrifying. But he was not terrified. He landed and made friends with them and explored in that wild country to see if he could find something which would be valuable enough to reimburse him for the expenses of the journey. And he found tin, Artaxerxes. And he stayed there for five years and mined it and brought home a ship load and sold it, and bought three other ships, and went back and worked for another five years and filled them all. He was a man of courage and enterprise." Her voice dropped several notes and she added casually, "I was reading about him this afternoon."

"And then you come to visit me . . . who am nothing more than the King of Persia. Oh, Esther, what a decline," Artaxerxes said. He laughed at the extravagance and then said: "Now I will tell you something. That Silashi of Tyre to whom you have lost your heart so completely was my great-great — oh, very remote grandfather. No, I am not boasting. I tell you, Esther, in good faith, that I have never mentioned this fact to anyone. My grandfather, when he conquered Tyre, fell in love with a woman of the people, the descendant of a family of crazy seamen who had wasted their substance on absurd ventures. He loved her and he married her, but in order to make her acceptable to his people he pretended that she was of noble birth. She subscribed to that legend until she was so old that she had lost her sense of decorum, and then, one day, when I was about ten years old, she told me the story of the Silashi of Tyre. I was a silly little boy, and though I was thrilled, as you have been thrilled by the achievements of my ancestors, I was also ashamed at having a common seaman and dyer for a great-great-great-grandfather. And now I am ashamed of being ashamed." He picked up his goblet and drank deeply. Esther said, "If I had those two men in my family, if I had that blood in my veins, I'd be so proud that I'd use the crown of Persia to play ball with."

He stared at her with a horror that was half affection and half genuine.

"I do mean it," she said. "Kings are made and unmade; the luck of war, the trend of politics, can hand a crown hither and thither. But the spirit of a man who can refrain from eating in order to grow a harvest that will carry him on, or face wild savages painted blue in order to satisfy his itch to explore, that is something no army, no politician can award. That spirit comes direct from God Himself. And if I say Majesty, or Lord, after this, Artaxerxes, I beg you to remember that in you I salute the blood of the Silashi of Tyre."

Through the pearly powder her flushed cheeks shone like a damask rose through the dew of morning, and her eyes were like stars. And then, suddenly, she remembered Mordecai and his careful schooling. She had failed him. Her spirits rushed downwards.

"I'm sorry," she said. "I have offended you. I should have remembered our relative positions. Have I your leave to retire?"

"Without supper?" Artaxerxes asked, picking up the golden bell and ringing it vigorously. "Oh no, Esther. A decree is a decree. And the decree reads that the visit should last out an evening. I have been bored, I have been repulsed — oh, that scent of musk — but I have adhered to my own rule. Tell me, in what book did you read the history of the Silashi?"

"In an old, very obscure book called *An Account of Various Voyages*. Doesn't that sound dull? It came from your own library, Artaxerxes, and Hegai was terrified lest I read it while I ate — a bad habit of mine — and marked it. But I was very careful."

"Where is it now?"

"In the room that was assigned to me."

Artaxerxes turned to the servant who had just entered bearing the first supper dish.

"Put that down," he said, "and go across and ask Hegai to bring me a scroll from the room which this lady occupies. Esther, where did you leave it?"

"It is the one nearest the pillow on the couch under the window," Esther said. "The scroll itself is yellowed, and the cord that ties it is blue and very much frayed. Nearest the pillow on the couch under the window, a yellowish scroll tied with blue cord. Can you remember that?"

A good manner, Artaxerxes thought — clear orders, not arrogantly given, pleasant, direct, incisive speech. When the servant had gone, obediently leaving the dish, covered as it was, upon the side table, the King of Persia, Lord of the Far Lands and Ruler of One Hundred and Twenty-seven Provinces, rose from his couch and with his own hands served, first, Esther, and then himself.

"And now," he said, sitting down comfortably beside her. "Tell me what else you have read during your captivity."

Esther thought for a moment and then remembered:

"Oh, one most remarkably entertaining story," she said. "But it came from a Jewish book, and perhaps you do not care for the Jews."

"I neither care nor do not care, if that makes sense to you," said Artaxerxes, halting his knife. "I know nothing of them, except that they have fine funerals," said the man into whose rule and dominion some tens of thousands of Jews had fallen. "Tell me the story."

"Well, there was once a man called Samson . . ." began Esther.

The servant returned with the scroll and other servants came in and out with dishes of fruit, dishes of meat, dishes of sweetmeats and dishes of rare delectable fruit. Finally came the little Nubian boys with silver bowls of rose-scented water and fine linen towels.

And then they came back with their torches and conducted Esther back across the garden to the Pavilion of Women, and there was something in the manner of their master when he took leave of this guest that infected their behaviour, so that they led this woman, who had no titles of her own, and no impressive robes or jewels, most gravely and respectfully.

Artaxerxes, left alone in his own apartment, thought deeply for a few moments and then summoned his steward.

"The test is completed," he said shortly. He was not going to betray himself. To say that for the first time in two years he had been taken out of himself, had forgotten that he was King of Persia, had even forgotten the banished, scornful Vashti. He said simply: "The test is completed. I have chosen the woman Esther. See you to all the arrangements for the wedding and the crowning."

The news was announced in Shushan next morning, and in the small bleak house in the Street of Camels, Mordecai fell to his knees and prayed, "Lord God of Abraham, Isaac, and of Jacob, strengthen Thou the weak hands of this woman that they may be strong in Thy cause."

CHAPTER
NINE

The morning after the Coronation, Hegai, with his seven hundred gold pieces and his life's savings in a bag, his title deeds in a scroll, and his personal effects loaded upon the backs of six mules, departed for his promised estate in Nineveh and Mordecai, lingering by the palace gateway, missed the familiar face, the by this time well-established exchange of remarks. So he opened a conversation with the porter himself, and so heard not only a full account of the glories of the Coronation, but of the fury with which the rest of the women had taken their dismissal.

"And however silly and trivial this matter may seem," said the porter, "it's likely to breed trouble. Because, you see, one of the women who never even got *near* Artaxerxes, who is naturally furious, was Bigthana's daughter — you know Bigthana, Lord of the Northern Gate." He threw out his hand to indicate Bigthana's domain. "And the odd thing is that this is the second time in a short space that Bigthana has been disappointed. He'd marked down the lordship of the Eastern Gate for his nephew, and the King gave it to Haman the Amalekite, and now Bigthana's daughter has been sent home without even being granted an interview."

"Very annoying for him," said Mordecai carefully.

"Annoying?" said the porter. "I should say so. All the more when you consider that on his *mother's* side he has a claim to the throne himself. We all know that the female side isn't taken into account. But when a man is set aside and sees his mother's brother's son held in such honour just because he is in the male succession — and then tries to make up for it and is defeated twice . . . well, it breeds bitterness," said the porter, and spat into the street.

"Bigthana attended the Coronation?"

"Oh yes. He carried one corner of the Queen's canopy. And his daughter, the Lady Eldava, was one of the Queen's attendants. But they weren't very happy — Corin told me."

"And who is Corin?"

"Corin is my cousin; he is steward to Bigthana. He says that Bigthana feels himself insulted, and that my Lord Teresh — his brother-in-law — sympathises with him, and that there'll be trouble eventually."

"It seems very possible," said Mordecai.

"That promotion of Haman," said the porter, lowering his voice, "was a bad move. He is an Amalekite, you know."

"But the Persians have no quarrel with the Amalekites," Mordecai said. And waited.

The porter seemed about to speak and then changed his mind.

82

"The Amalekites are hated by everybody," he said at last.

And you're a Jew — though you pretend; though you won't admit it, Mordecai thought. Only a Jew could say the word "Amalekite" in that accusing, condemnatory way. I shall cultivate your acquaintance.

And from that time onwards, for several weeks, Mordecai was to be seen lingering by the palace gate gossiping with his friend the porter. Occasionally there was a third in the group, the porter's cousin Corin, a well-informed fellow with a sharp ear, a keen eye, and a shrewd mind.

Mordecai, who missed talking to Esther and arguing with her, and had been lonely through the past months, enjoyed these little meetings with his cronies, and was also thus assured of hearing, at first hand, any news of Esther.

He never mentioned that he was the Queen's uncle, and now that the choice was made and Hegai gone to his estate, there was no one to connect the shabby old Jew outside the palace gateway with the lovely young Queen within.

One evening, when Esther had been on the throne for about six months, Mordecai and the porter were gossiping by the gate when Corin arrived, pale green in the face and with his lively eyes standing out from his head like a terrified hare's.

"What ails you, Corin?" asked the porter. "Why, man, you look as though you'd seen a ghost. Here, sit down." He dragged forward a little stool and forced his cousin to sit down upon it, asking again what was the matter.

"Nothing, nothing," said Corin, "at least nothing that I can tell you. I can't tell anybody, that's the trouble."

"Rubbish," said the porter briskly, "we're all friends here I should hope and need have no secrets. If you're in debt again, you extravagant rascal — well, I helped you last time, didn't I? Yes," he added, turning to Mordecai, "I, a poor porter with nothing but my miserable pay and a tip or two now and then, had to dip into my savings to save this worthless cousin of mine from a debtor's fate — and he the steward to the great Lord Bigthana."

"I happen to be an honest steward," said Corin, wiping his dry mouth with his unsteady hand. "I've always served my Lord well and faithfully, but now I don't know where my duty lies and that's the truth."

"Well, if it isn't your debts, what is it?" the porter asked with friendly roughness. Corin moaned out again that it was something too terrible to mention.

"Not your health?" Corin shook his head.

Mordecai, sitting with his hands tucked into his sleeves and his eyes watchful, said, "Some wine might help to restore him."

"Ah," said the porter, "but the trouble is I can't watch folks drinking without wanting to drink myself, and I mustn't drink on duty. However, within ten minutes I shall be relieved. Then we'll step across to my house, Corin, and share the wine-skin that is cooling in my well-mouth. You come too, my friend." Mordecai gravely accepted the invitation.

As soon as the night-porter came on duty the three men went across to the porter's house. The porter himself seemed little concerned with his cousin's state and busied himself with drawing up the wine-skin, setting out the cups and bringing cakes and fruit from the kitchen. But Mordecai watched Corin closely and saw that the man was suffering from genuine shock. He remembered the porter's casual reference, during their first conversation, to the discontent felt by Corin's master over the East Gate wardenship and the choice of Queen, and it struck him as just possible that the man, if he cared to talk now, might reveal something of interest and importance. So he waited. Wine, the ancients said, "maketh glad the heart of a man" . . . it also loosened tongues.

Corin drank a cupful and then another, and the pale green colour left his face and his eyes resumed their normal position. But still he said nothing.

"Ah, you look better now," said his cousin, smacking his own lips appreciatively. "That was good wine, wasn't it? I took the precaution of putting another skin to cool when I lifted this one. So drink away my friends. And now, Corin, what mares' nest have you stumbled on this time? He's such an excitable fellow, you know. That time when he wanted to borrow my savings he didn't ask, you know. He came to me and talked about hanging himself — the fool. I had to worm it out of him then. Here, Corin, fill up, and tell us what made you run round looking like a lunatic."

Corin said again, "I daren't tell you." Then he picked up the cup, his third, emptied it at a draught, set it down and burst into drunken tears. "It all arose," he blurted, "from listening at doors"; but then he always *had* listened at doors. Bigthana was so forgetful and unpractical that many times Corin had saved him from a bad bargain, or from being made a fool of by being able to tell him just what was said at some interview which was supposed to have been private. "If I'm there in the room," he sobbed, "people know that they can't take advantage of him; so often I stay outside and listen and they speak freely, and then I remind him later on, or know things without being told. In fact I have always regarded listening at doors as part of my duty."

"Well," said the porter, "this time you listened and heard him say you were a bad steward and he was going to sack you. Is that it?"

"Oh no," said Corin simply, wiping his face with his sleeve, "I'd know what to do then. Everybody knows I'm a good steward, I could easily find a place. Now I don't know what to do."

"Well, if you don't tell us we can't advise you," said the porter, who seemed oddly lacking in real curiosity. "I'll get that other skin and we'll drink and drown our sorrows, real and imaginary." Corin put his arms on the table and laid his head on them and moaned. But he drank again when his cousin filled up his cup. Then all at once he was truly drunk, past the tearful stage, prepared to be communicative. "He . . ." he said, indicating his cousin, "has a good heart but no head. Now you," he said, looking into Mordecai's face and wildly trying to focus his eyes, "are a clever man. A scholar. You tell me what you'd do in my case."

"I'd have to know what your case is before I could advise you," said Mordecai, concealing his excitement.

"It's this . . ." said Corin, and suddenly the words bubbled out, faster than he could speak them clearly, so that Mordecai, and the now-interested porter, had to lean closer to hear. And he told them that his master, Bigthana, was plotting together with Teresh, his brother-in-law, whose son had failed to be made Lord of the Eastern Gate, to assassinate Artaxerxes.

"Absolute rubbish," said the porter, now a little tipsy himself. "Look here, I've been on that gate now for fifteen years. I hear all the gossip. There hasn't been a week when somebody isn't threatening to kill somebody. 'I'll kill him for this . . .' everybody says it. It's the way the nobility talk. Your master is cross because his daughter didn't even have a chance to show her paces, and Teresh is cross because his son wasn't made Warden. So they get together and say, 'We'll kill him for this — the rogue.' But they mean nothing. You are a silly fellow, Corin. By the gods I thought you had something serious on your mind."

"He'sh the fool," said Corin, slurring his words. "Now you, shir, are a shenshible man. What would you do?" He turned to Mordecai, who was entirely sober; he had sipped his first cup of wine, and the porter had hospitably filled up the cup to the brim; after that, seeing the cup full again he had passed it over in his dispensations. The good, incisive brain behind Mordecai's watchful eyes was clear and unmuddled. He thought rapidly and gave his answer without noticeable hesitation.

"I should do nothing, Corin. The quarrels of the great do not concern us. What your master does is his own affair, and in this case you are not supposed even to know his plans. If this matter concerned your stewardship . . . a matter of rents or charges or work to be done, then you should do your duty and admit your knowledge. But this is a matter outside your stewardship."

"But Artashershes," said Corin, making a sad mess of the name, "is quite a nische man. Bit shilly, perhapsh, but for a man in hish poshition, nische. Thatsh what bothersh me. On the other hand, if I managed to warn him — and how I would do that I can't think — I'm betraying my own mashter. It'sh enough to drive a man crashy," he said.

"There is not the slightest need for you to do anything," said Mordecai. "The matter can safely be left . . ." he hesitated for a moment and then risked it, "to Jehovah," he finished. Corin, who had carefully concealed his nationality in order to become Bigthana's steward, and the porter who went regularly with his fellow servants to worship in the temple of Astaroth — the goddess most fashionable in Shushan at the moment — stared at him, shocked into soberness.

"Great is our God and greatly to be praised," said Mordecai.

"Bless the Lord, oh my soul, and all that is within me, bless His holy name," responded the porter, and Corin, remembering the ritual that they had learned at their mothers' knees: remembering, oh, remembering, a thousand things ... the vanished greatness of their race, the glories of Jerusalem, the conquests of David, the wisdom of Solomon ... all the stories past, the legends, the glittering pageant of their national history.

"If I forget thee, oh Jerusalem, let my right hand forget her cunning; if I do not remember thee, let my tongue cleave to the roof of my mouth; if I prefer not Jerusalem above my chief joy," said Mordecai, quoting the poem brought from Babylon by one of his race.

The three of them, having at last admitted their origin, having admitted the thing that had drawn them together, could have gone on quoting and confessing and talking all night. But Mordecai, after a few minutes, excused himself, saying he had a letter which must be written that evening. He had been perfectly honest when he had told Corin to take no action, to leave the matter to Jehovah; but he had been equally honest when, some months earlier, he had explained that Jehovah worked through His tools. To Mordecai it was all beautifully simple; he had happened to make friends with the porter and the porter's cousin happened to be Bigthana's steward, and he had happened to listen at a door and tell what he had heard, and Mordecai had happened to be present and Esther happened to be Queen of Persia; and so it would happen that Esther would be able to warn the King of the plot, and in the time when the Jews happened to be in danger, Artaxerxes would happen to remember that once Esther had saved his life and he would happen to listen to her pleas for her people. Happen, happen,

happen — what a loose term for the hand of God, Mordecai thought as he let himself into his own house and settled down to his writing.

CHAPTER
TEN

When Esther woke in the morning it was always to find a slave standing by her bedside with a silver tray. On the tray was a silver goblet dimmed by the contrast between the warm atmosphere of the room and the chill of the fruit juice which had been all night suspended down the well. For a little while it had seemed very strange and slightly wrong to lean back against the pillows and sip the cool juice while other slaves ran backwards and forwards preparing her bath and then, with exquisite timing, bringing her breakfast; but the strangeness had worn off during the time when she had waited for her turn for Artaxerxes' inspection and now, except to think that it was very pleasant, she hardly noticed the morning's routine.

This morning, lying beside the mist-dimmed goblet was a piece of papyrus, folded and sealed. She recognised it at once, with a pang, with a smile. Papyrus was expensive and Mordecai was poor, and one day he had come back from the market very pleased by a bargain he had picked up; thirty-six sheets of papyrus written over on one side and perfectly clean on the other, which had been thrown out from some merchant house and salvaged by a rag picker. Mordecai and Esther had used the clean sides and ignored the others until one day he had said, "There must be some way of cleaning this stuff — it confuses me to turn a page and read about a bale of cloth being charged to someone's account five years ago. What would clean it, Esther?"

She had thought futilely for a moment and then said, "Fuller's earth bleaches linen. It might work on papyrus."

And it had, to an extent; the old writing in some places remained stubborn and was not easy to write over, but the cloth merchant's transactions did fade out and it was just possible to use both sides of the sheets. Now, in the Palace of Shushan where clean new papyrus, smelling of Egypt, was to be had for the asking, Esther recognised the old, blotched piece, and knew that Mordecai had written to her at last. His letters had been very rare of late.

She broke the seal and spread the page and then gave a half-humorous, half-exasperated sigh. It was written in their own private cypher. Mordecai had invented it, long ago, when she was a little girl, nine years old, and had come across the word "his private cypher" in a history book. She had asked Mordecai to explain, and he had explained as he explained everything, with immense thoroughness. He had said, "Now suppose we invent our own private cypher," and he had juggled with letters and scribbled for a time and then explained it to her; and for a day or two they had communicated by means of the cypher, a very simple one, once you knew the key. But that was six — no, seven — years ago; and Mordecai, before sitting down to write, had doubtless consulted the key; Esther had forgotten it, and for five minutes stared at the sheet completely baffled. Then she thought, it would begin with my name . . . Mordecai always opened his letters with the words "My dear Esther" . . . now . . . Painfully, letter by letter, she relearned the key and deciphered the letter and learned, with astonishment mingled with incredulity, that there was a plot afoot for the assassination of her husband. The words finally seemed to leap from the page and shout at her. Somebody was planning to kill Artaxerxes.

It was at that moment that she realised that she loved him. She had then been his wife for rather over six months. She had been forced by Mordecai and her own sense of duty into entering the contest for queenship, and almost staggered when she learned that Artaxerxes had chosen her. The wedding and the Coronation had had a dream-like quality, and she had never had, until this moment, any sense of unity such as, she supposed, should exist between husbands and wives. He had been very kind, always; immensely considerate, entertaining, amusing. But she had always thought of him as something apart from herself; had remembered that she must entertain and amuse him, that she must look her best for him, please him. As though he were a stranger whom she was meeting for the first time.

And now, learning that he was in danger, it seemed as though she herself were threatened. Everything affectionate and protective in her rose to the surface. She leaped out of bed, and with one hand warded off the attentive slave while with the other she snatched her slippers and the robe which she wore in her bathroom. Then, with untouched face, unbrushed hair, just as she had left her bed, she raced away, through anterooms and corridors, across the garden, where the dew still misted the grass, through more corridors and anterooms until she reached Artaxerxes' private apartments and the copper door, inlaid with ivory and silver which had opened to Hegai's signal six months earlier.

Artaxerxes was not alone. Early as it was, Haman and Zethar and Harbonah were present, earnestly discussing some matter; and a number of slaves hovered in the background. The bed was strewn with tablets and sheets of papyrus and a slave, bringing in the breakfast, had to clear a place before he set it down. At the opening of the big door every eye in the place turned towards it, and Esther was suddenly conscious of her dishevelment. But her news was of more importance than her appearance, and she ran forward, falling on her knees by the bedside and crying "My Lord, I crave a moment's speech in private with you."

The courtiers stepped back with grave ironic smiles; Artaxerxes looked slightly shamed and apologetic.

"I offer you the morning's greetings," he said, formally, which reminded her that she had omitted them.

"I am sorry to enter your presence uninvited and unannounced, my Lord," she said hastily — thinking what nonsense it all was. Here was a man in danger of his life and one had to apologise for coming to tell him

94

so. "I have a matter of the utmost importance to communicate to you."

"It must be *very* important," said Artaxerxes, whimsically surveying her attire and her ruffled hair.

"Oh, it is, is it? Send these people away, please."

Artaxerxes, with an expression that said, allow me to humour her, after all we have only been married a short time, signed to his gentlemen to retire; but he said within their hearing before they reached the door: "Look here, my dear, we were discussing something extremely important, the new uniform for the tenth archery division." And Esther said in a voice that was equally audible: "That isn't so important, Artaxerxes, as what I have to tell you." His lips folded over one another in the expression of a man summoning patience. The door behind Haman and the others closed, and Esther said: "Do you think I would force myself upon you thus for something of less importance than the archers' new uniform? I came to warn you that two men you trust, Bigthana and Teresh, are planning to assassinate you."

Artaxerxes threw himself back against his pillow and roared with laughter. "So I picked myself another dreamer of dreams," he spluttered, and then checked himself, remembering that Vashti shouldn't be mentioned, even indirectly, to Esther. But Vashti had sometimes mentioned her dreams and the far-fetched interpretations of them, and it seemed to him at that moment that here was another resemblance between his old love and his new. "So you dreamed that poor old Bigthana murdered me, did you, Esther?"

"I didn't dream it," Esther said. "This afternoon Bigthana and Teresh are going to hunt gazelle with you. At one moment Teresh will ride up beside you and point, saying, 'Did you see that, my Lord?' and Bigthana will shoot. The arrow is poisoned and will strike you in the temple as you turn your head." She had begun to speak in a mood of irritation, but as she proceeded she saw his sceptical expression change to one of incredulous surprise, rather like that of a pampered little boy who learns suddenly that someone dislikes him. And at that her heart moved in her breast and, going forward to the bed, she cried: "Oh, do take heed, Artaxerxes. Don't go with them. Believe me; please believe me. Send for them now and accuse them."

Artaxerxes had recovered himself. "Where did you get this incredible story, Esther?"

"Does that matter?"

"Most certainly it does. You are still so new to palace life, my dear, you could hardly be expected to realise that jealousy and intrigue are the rule here. Any enemy of Bigthana might plant that tale — on the principle that at least some suspicion would remain in my mind even if he cleared himself when accused. Do you understand? Therefore it is important to know where the story arose."

"It isn't part of palace intrigue. I would stake my life, Artaxerxes, on the truthfulness and integrity of the person who sent me the information."

He began to look thoughtful. "It is possible, I suppose. But why was the information sent to you?"

"To make sure that it reached you in time. Who else," she asked wryly, "would have dared to burst in and disturb you . . ."

". . . in the middle of a discussion about archers' uniforms?" finished Artaxerxes, and burst out laughing. "Quite true. Everybody else is so law-abiding that they would let me be knifed sooner than interrupt a conference."

"Now that you know, what are you going to do? Arrest them?"

"No, no, my dear. What would that serve? They would deny it all, and whoever betrayed them to your informant would withdraw the story and we'd be just where we are. I have a better idea. I shall go gazelle hunting this afternoon, if Bigthana invites me, and I shall most obligingly turn my head if Teresh draws my attention to anything, and then . . ." he smiled, this time with a grim smile.

"And then?" Esther asked anxiously.

"They will be caught in the act; no argument possible."

"But you . . . Oh, Artaxerxes, it sounds a dangerous plan. Suppose you weren't careful, or quick enough? You mustn't die in order to prove their guilt."

"Don't worry," said Artaxerxes. He reached out his hand and, putting it under her chin, turned her face to his. "You are worried. Sweet child. I believe you really care what happens to me."

"Of course I do," Esther said.

"Have you had your breakfast? No. Well, sit down and share mine. No, everything is spoilt, what was hot is tepid and what was cold is warm." He clapped his hands. Haman, and Zethar and Harbonah appeared in the doorway thinking he had summoned them back to continue the discussion.

"Go away," said Artaxerxes bluntly, "and order me a fresh breakfast and more of it. The Queen has graciously consented to share the meal with me."

Zethar, who privately approved of Esther, not because he liked her for herself, but because her success with Artaxerxes was a tribute to the cleverness of his own method of choosing a new Queen, smiled tolerantly; Harbonah, who had breakfasted early, felt that the postponement offered a good chance of snatching some refreshment; but Haman, who had been on the point of making one of his wittiest and most flattering remarks when this untidy female burst in, scowled and looked at his Queen with hatred. Lately Haman had flattered himself that his power over Artaxerxes was unlimited, and unequalled; it was galling to be sent out to wait while the Queen took breakfast with the King. Women should be kept in their place.

The plot was not mentioned again until the meal was over. Then Esther ventured to repeat her admonition to be careful. Artaxerxes promised to be very careful. Then he kissed and dismissed her and Esther went back to her own apartments.

It seemed a long day. Late in the afternoon a slave whom she had sent to keep watch, reported that the King had ridden out, dressed for hunting, accompanied by the Lords Bigthana and Teresh.

98

"No one else?" Esther asked.

"No one else," said the slave. "Perhaps my lady does not know that occasionally the King and the great Lords like to hunt, informally, pretending to be private gentlemen for the space of an afternoon."

"Go back, now," she said, "and keep good watch. Tell me the moment my Lord comes home."

Time moved heavily. She tried to take comfort by remembering Uncle Mordecai's words about everything being in the hand of God. And it must, she thought, have been the hand of God at work, for Mordecai to have come into possession of knowledge of the plot. How else could a quiet, scholarly old Jew in the humble Street of Camels know anything of the plans of great lords?

She prayed a little; grew hopeful; knew a fresh wave of depression. It grew late. The swift darkness came down and the slave posted to report did not return. She sent another to seek him. Artaxerxes had not returned. Presently she grew desperate; she knew what had happened. Bigthana and Teresh had succeeded in their plan and killed the King; but they dared not come riding back in triumph to the royal city of Shushan, where Artaxerxes was very popular; they had gone off with their story making it sound like an accident, or a shrewd political move, to one of the subject cities — Babylon or Nineveh . . . where any anti-royalist action was sure to find some supporters. And Artaxerxes, whom she loved, was dead . . . dead . . . It was impossible to be hopeful any more. Mordecai had failed her, Jehovah had failed her. She lay down on a divan and sobbed until her eyes were swollen and her whole face soggy and her head aching violently.

She had given orders that no-one save the slave who was watching was to enter the room until she rang her silver bell. So no one came to draw the curtains, or to bring the candles or food. The moon rose and cast long silver arrows into the room, and still she lay on the divan and sobbed.

All suddenly the door opened and she started up. "What news?" she cried sharply. "Has he returned safely? Speak, speak quickly."

"He has returned," said a voice — no slave's voice. The King's own voice, merry and confident, the voice of a man who had scored a triumph and come to tell about it. Esther threw herself towards him, like a puppy whose master has left it alone overlong.

"Oh, my Lord, my Lord. You are safe. Thank God, thank God."

"I am safe. And why are you in the dark, Esther?"

"I thought you were dead. It is so late," she said, giving way again to tears, this time of relief and joy.

"It is late," he said, putting his arm about her and leading her back to the divan. "But there was much to do. Shall I tell you?"

"Please."

"Well, all went as arranged. I rode out with them and everything was merry. Thanks to your warning I had men posted — some to watch and some to act. At the critical moment, just as you said, Bigthana fell behind and Teresh, riding beside me, drew my attention, so that I should turn my head. There were six honest men to swear that he drew my attention to nothing; and six more who saw that Bigthana aimed at *me*, not at some mythical animal. I lay down along my horse's neck and the arrow passed over. Then my men pounced. We tested the arrow on a coney and it was poisoned, as you said. We held the trial there and then. Properly, for all officials had been warned and were there in the woods, waiting. The trial was all in order, farcical, of course because their guilt was self-evident. But it was a correct legal trial and they were found guilty and hanged. That is why I am so late." He tightened his arm about her and said, "I owe you my life." And then he added inconsequently, "I am most exceedingly hungry."

"So am I," said Esther. "I have been unable to eat all day. Now I could eat two banquets."

"Let's try," cried Artaxerxes. "I'll order a banquet for eight, and you and I and Haman and that lady, Zeresh, to whom he's taken a fancy, shall sit down to it and see who can eat most."

"Must we have Haman and Zeresh?" Esther asked.

"I think so. Haman is such good company, and he was extraordinarily good and active this afternoon. You've only seen him officially, when he pretends to be very stately, an absolute sobersides — but at a party . . . well, you'll see."

The moonlight was now brilliant in the room and Esther could see her husband's face, smooth and happy as a child's. He was delighted with his afternoon's adventure; delighted by the thought of a party. This was no moment to say that she loathed, distrusted, feared his favourite, Haman, and the woman it looked as though he would marry.

"We'll have a party," she agreed, "if I can get my face into anything like shape."

"As it is," said Artaxerxes tenderly, rather gloating over the fact that she had cried herself into ugliness on his account, "it is the prettiest face in the world." He kissed it and then jumped to his feet. "I must have a bath. Be ready in an hour."

The feast was a great success. Esther, trying to be just, admitted to herself that Haman was extremely amusing — without being a clown exactly he contributed just that element of nonsense and foolery which a professional fool would have done. He was a very clever mimic and Artaxerxes, who after all suffered a great deal from court etiquette and from pompous courtiers, laughed until he cried at Haman's brilliant imitations of old Zethar, Harbonah and Carcas.

"And now," said Haman at one point, "I'll show you, my Lord, what you look like when you have to receive a distasteful deputation and are obliged to give them your attention. May I borrow the crown for a moment?"

Artaxerxes obligingly took off the slender, diamond-studded circle which he wore on all informal occasions and handed it to Haman, who set it straight on his own head, folded his arms, and looked very solemn. He mimed the deputation — it was something about irrigation in some desert place, and he mimed Artaxerxes getting more and more bored and fidgety. It was a brilliant performance, even Esther could see that; but it was cruel and it was mocking. He scratched his head and the crown slipped lopsided; he yawned and let his mouth stay a little open. Artaxerxes now and again protested: "No, no, Haman, I never act as badly as that. Oh, surely I never look like that . . ." But he laughed and laughed. And Esther, whose true Jewish gravity was shot by true Jewish wit and leavened with irony, thought — oh, but how can you let him make a fool of you? Can't you see that he's mocking you all the time?

Haman took off the crown, spun it like a hoop on his hand and sent it sailing through the air — as people threw wooden hoops for trinkets at a fair. "Caught you," he cried. "Now you belong to me, my Lord. My trophy."

"That's the second time to-day I have been aimed at," said Artaxerxes, settling the crown back on his head. And then suddenly he was grave and dignified again. Turning to Esther he said:

"By the way, will you give me the name of your informant. I'm sorry I have forgotten to ask until now. I owe my life to him — and to you. He must be rewarded."

"His name," said Esther slowly, "is Mordecai. *Mordecai*. And he lives in the Street of Camels." She would have been very glad, and very proud, at that moment to have added that he was her uncle, the man who had brought her up. But Mordecai himself had forbidden her, very strictly, and giving reasons, to mention that fact.

"You have your tablets," Artaxerxes said, turning around to Haman. It was one of Haman's peculiarities that he always carried his writing materials . . . the little service which sometimes meant so much. "Make a note of that, will you. I want it to be included in the official record of to-day's affair. And if I forget, you might remind me about the reward. A thousand gold pieces and some honour . . . Is this man poor, Esther?"

"Very poor."

"Some title then that carries an income with it. I'll look into that to-morrow. Meantime, let's drink to his outlandish name. Mordecai . . . to Mordecai, protector of the throne."

CHAPTER
ELEVEN

Haman prided himself on not hastily jumping to conclusions. It might not be the same man. One must wait and investigate. But as he wrote the name *Mordecai* on his tablet and put it away he saw, with the extreme clarity of hatred, a grave, bearded Jewish face.

He had noticed this particular Mordecai some time before, near the palace gate; on the morning, in fact, after his own patent of nobility had been publicly announced. That had been a wonderful morning. Everyone had bowed to the new-made noble, anxious to show him honour. The old Jew had not bowed, and Haman had thought — perhaps he can't read, or is deaf, and so hasn't heard the news of my nobility; on the other hand, he can *see* and he might do as the others do out of imitation if nothing else . . .

But some mornings later, when everyone in Shushan and everyone in any town and village the couriers had reached, knew that Haman was now a lord and entitled to full honours, there the old Jew had been again, near the palace gate when Haman emerged; and he hadn't bowed his head or doffed his old hat, and as Haman drew level with him he saw that the old man's eyes looked through him unseeingly. Haman had paused that time by the porter's lodge and asked, "Who is that old fellow?"

"His name is Mordecai, my Lord."

"He isn't blind, is he?"

"No. He is a scholar, my Lord, and very absent-minded."

Haman grunted and passed on. And the porter had said to Mordecai, his friend: "His new lordship likes salutes. I told him you were very absent-minded."

"I shall continue to be so," said Mordecai. "The only way an Amalekite can make me bow my head would be to cut if off at the neck."

The porter, as a palace servant, was bound to show respect to the new-made lord, so he felt uncomfortable and let the matter drop. And since Mordecai was often now at the palace gateway and Haman often going in and out, the situation was often repeated. Always to Haman's chagrin.

On the morning after Artaxerxes' escape from assassination Haman went several times to the palace gateway and at last found Mordecai paying his morning visit to the porter. The visit was of some importance to Mordecai, who had been anxious to know whether his letter to Esther had borne fruit. The porter was telling him all about it when Haman appeared. The porter stopped his story and bowed and said: "The morning's greetings, my Lord." Mordecai stood straight and stared into the remote distance. Haman swung round.

"I believe that your name is Mordecai."

"You believe correctly."

"And you live in the Street of Camels?"

"That is so."

"Does any other of your name reside there?"

"Not to my knowledge."

Haman grunted and passed on.

"Now you've offended him again," said the porter. "Well, as I was telling you . . . something must have leaked out or the King had a suspicion. They say that he lay down absolutely flat on his horse as though he knew what was coming . . ."

Haman went into the palace: first to the scribes' room, where diligent clerks were writing down the official accounts of the previous day's events. The chief clerk greeted him humbly.

"My Lord, His Majesty the King says that you have a record of the name of the informer who set this plot at nought. His Majesty has forgotten how the name is spelt. Perhaps you would be so kind as to inform us. We have left a space."

"The name is spelled M-o-r-d-e-c-a-i," said Haman. "Oh, and by the way, I have a suggestion to make. I don't think this record should go into the ordinary rack. His Majesty makes light of the affair, but it isn't very pleasant for a King to know that two of his subjects planned to assassinate him. It would be tactful to suppress the whole thing. The account must be written, of course, but then, if I were you, I would put it aside somewhere and let it be forgotten. Lay it with all those unpleasant old records of Mirimah's rebellion."

"Very good, my Lord," said the chief scribe, regretting that he had wasted so much good penmanship. He filled in the name Mordecai in the space he had left, sealed the scroll, and tossed it on to the top of the cupboard where the records of a forgotten little rebellion lay gathering the dust.

Haman passed on towards the King's apartments. And presently after some attempts to raise a smiling response from his favourite, Artaxerxes said: "Haman, what ails you. Did you eat or drink too much last night? Or are you sorry that Bigthana didn't carry out his plan?"

"I am depressed," Haman said. "I can't help not being of noble blood, can I? And until lately the King's patent of nobility was enough to guarantee respect. Now it isn't. There are people in the street who do not salute me or do me honour or address me respectfully. And that insults you as well as me, and makes me fear for your authority. What with yesterday's affair and the contempt I met with this morning, I do feel depressed."

"It can't be a general revolutionary feeling," said Artaxerxes. "I've never heard any other noble complain of lack of honour."

"No. That is what troubles me. Zethar and the rest were born noble — and the people respect them. I was made . . . and when common people fail to do me honour it reflects upon you, my Lord, as though the King had no longer power to make a man noble. Do you see what I mean.? For myself, I don't care. I don't mind whether they doff their greasy caps or not . . . but it is a straw which shows the way the wind is blowing."

"I'll see to that," Artaxerxes said. "Perhaps it wasn't quite clear; people are so stupid. I just gave you a title

108

and an estate and left the rest to chance. It was my fault, my dear Haman; please forgive me. I will to-day issue a decree, specifically stating that you . . ." — he laughed suddenly — "are to take precedence of all princes. That will show them whether I can or cannot make a man a noble. Haman, I'll decree that after me you are to be the first man in the kingdom. Send the chief scribe now; we'll have the decree posted this afternoon.

And now, he thought, my dear Haman, resume your good humour and cheer me up, for I overdrank and overate yesterday, and need cheering this morning. Haman, to whom the news that he was to be set above all princes was fantastically in excess of his wildest hopes, found no difficulty in being cheerful and in making his master laugh.

In the midst of his laughter Artaxerxes said suddenly: "And by the way, if you really have a fancy for Zeresh, you'd better marry her soon. She is, after all, supremely well connected and, together with the decree, should establish you satisfactorily."

Haman's cup was full to overflowing. For some time now he had wanted to marry Zeresh, but had hesitated to suggest it, fearing that both she, and Artaxerxes, to whom she was remotely related, might think the proposal presumption on his part. Now Artaxerxes himself had suggested it.

The sudden triumph rushed to his head. Suddenly it seemed that there was no limit to what he could attain.

He looked back and saw himself a menial, carrying torches, serving at table, being entrusted with some small errand and gaining a small promotion; making the King laugh by a well-timed remark and being rewarded; the story of his small advancements reached backwards like a piece of careful embroidery, move on move, stitch on stitch. And now, with apparent suddenness, the whole careful pattern was revealed in all its glory. Second only to the King of all Persia . . . married to Zeresh.

He was quite dazzled by what he had achieved.

That afternoon Artaxerxes' decree was posted in all the usual places. From that time henceforward Haman was to be treated with all honour due to the first Prince of the land. And within a week Haman's name was prominent again; he was married, with every possible ceremony and pomp, to Zeresh. Artaxerxes, for a wedding gift, bestowed a new title, another estate and an enormous ornate palace near the city's centre. Esther was compelled to kiss the bride and call her "Cousin," and hang her own gift, a string of perfectly matched pearls, about her neck. And there was nothing lacking in Haman's happiness until, four days after his wedding, he chanced to encounter Mordecai near the palace gateway.

CHAPTER
TWELVE

He was wildly ambitious, colossally conceited, but he was not without commonsense, and throughout that whole day he kept asking himself what did it matter, reminding himself that it did not, *could* not matter. And yet again and again he found himself thinking about this one single person who would not salute him, would not give the honour due. Just a stupid old Jew, very shabby, obviously poor, a person of no importance at all. Why should it matter to Haman — rich, noble, second only to the King — whether such a creature doffed his cap and bowed or not? It shouldn't, couldn't, didn't matter.

Yet it did. For the truth was that each time Haman met Mordecai and faced that grave, unseeing stare something happened; the honours shrivelled; the jewels turned into bits of glass; and Haman knew that he owed his honours, not to his cleverness, but to the fact that he had managed to relieve the King's boredom for a little while; and he knew that Zeresh had married him for the sake of his position; and he knew that he was only a smart, self-seeking Amalekite; and he knew that what goes up suddenly often comes down the same way. Every time Mordecai looked at Haman and failed to grovel to him he held up the mirror to Haman's self. That was why it mattered.

It grew to be an obsession with him. He would remain in the palace until he saw Mordecai arrive for his evening gossip with the porter; then he would emerge, walking with dignity, very graciously acknowledging the salutes of the porter and anyone else who happened to be near. But the salutes of the others had no value. All he wanted, because it seemed to be the one thing that he could not command, was the reverence of this one old shabby Jew.

Even the cheerful porter noticed.

"You know, my friend," he said, a little timidly, "you're going clean against the law. The King expressly commanded that the Lord Haman should be given the reverence due to himself. If he chose to turn nasty you'd find yourself in a queer spot."

"If it had been the will of Jehovah that I should do reverence to an Amalekite then He would have let the Amalekites win the battle of Edzana. Nebuchadnezzar defeated Israel — therefore it is the will of Jehovah that we should bow ourselves before the Babylonians. Cyrus of Persia conquered Babylon and Jehovah did not stir. We were handed over, to work out our destiny under the Persians.

"To Artaxerxes, who inherited from Cyrus, I will, if I must, do reverence. But why should I reverence an Amalekite upstart? Besides, it rather amuses me to watch him squirm and wonder. And, apart from that, he is the acknowledged enemy of our people. I will not salute him."

"Please yourself," said the cheerful porter. "But if trouble comes, don't say I didn't warn you."

"Trouble will come," said Mordecai gravely, "even though I fall on my face and lick the dust before the Amalekite's feet."

Fortunately for his peace of mind, Mordecai never realised how much his own stubborn behaviour contributed to hastening the trouble. Nobody in Shushan or in the one hundred and twenty-seven provinces would have believed that one old Jew's failure to doff his cap and do reverence could result in a plot to exterminate a whole race. And perhaps it is hardly fair to attribute to Mordecai's action the responsibility for Haman's. For the Jews and the Amalekites were enemies of such long standing that nowhere where a Jew was in power could an Amalekite long survive, and nowhere where an Amalekite held sway could a Jew hope for more than a swift and easy death. Sooner or later Haman was bound to move against his old enemies; but when he did so he saw, not the hundreds of humble little artisans and craftsmen, the inoffensive women and children, but the one Jew who represented them in his distorted vision, the single stubborn old man who would not doff his cap.

Meanwhile, Haman, though he did not immediately realise the fact, had scored a minor triumph; he had come between Artaxerxes and Esther. The quarrel had arisen in the simplest way, as quarrels do, and had its origin, if only the King could have realised it, in her love for him. For the one thing that a woman who loves a man cannot bear to see is for him to be made to look

113

ridiculous. And Esther, who did not share Artaxerxes' infatuated appreciation for Haman's clowning, could very clearly see that behind that clowning there was the mockery, the encroachment.

Soon after Haman and Zeresh were married they gave a feast, which Esther and Artaxerxes attended. It was a feast of the utmost magnificence, and Haman was in his most amusing mood, and Artaxerxes enjoyed every moment of it; even the charade, in which Haman played the part of King Solomon and Artaxerxes, with his face blacked with burnt cork and limping from a supposedly deformed foot, was cast for the part of the Queen of Sheba who, at first confident and arrogant, was overcome by Solomon's wisdom and grandeur, and eventually left for her own country "with no more spirit in her." Artaxerxes threw himself into his part with a will, and so did Haman; and Esther, watching, reminded herself that it was only a play; only a charade.

But a few days later Artaxerxes said that he must return the feast. And Esther said, incautiously: "If it could be just a feast, just an entertainment . . . not a chance for Haman to exhibit himself . . ."

"What on earth do you mean?"

"Well," she said slowly, trying to remain cool and impersonal, "at the feast, just before he was married, he played hoop-la with your crown; at the last one there was that charade . . ."

"And what was wrong with that?" He knew that he had looked a bit silly with his cork-blackened face, his limping gait, and his skirt contrived out of a piece of

114

curtain, but it was all amongst friends and all good fun. He wouldn't be criticised by his *wife*.

"Not wrong. Unseemly," Esther said. "In themselves these things amount to nothing; but there is something about Haman, a fundamental lack of respect. Oh, it is difficult to explain, but I always feel that he *enjoys* making you look silly. If it just happened, if he didn't set himself out to do it, it wouldn't matter; but I am perfectly sure that everything he says and does on these occasions is aimed at undermining your dignity . . . in a very subtle way."

"I never heard such arrant nonsense," said Artaxerxes, affronted, not so much by what she said as by the sneaking suspicion that she might be right. "Haman is the best and the most loyal of all my friends. And even a King must have some relaxation."

"I know," said Esther. She began to fumble for words which would exactly, and if possible without offence, convey her meaning. "I'm not saying that you behave in an undignified manner, Artaxerxes; in some company you could crawl on the floor and still remain King of Persia . . . I do know that dignity doesn't depend entirely on stiff behaviour. But Haman deliberately sets himself out to belittle you. When he borrowed your crown and gave that very amusing impersonation of being bored by a deputation — that wasn't enough; he had to scratch his head and set the crown crooked, and yawn and leave his mouth lolling open — mocking, making you look silly. And to-night, I don't suppose you noticed, but every one of the funny stories he told — and they were funny, I admit, because he is very clever — every single one of those stories, if you remember, was of somebody scoring off a King. There was the story of Nebuchadnezzar and the slave girl; the story of Cyrus and the beggar; the story of Cephalus and the fisherman — in every one of them the *King* came off worst and was made to look ridiculous. Do you think that was just coincidence?"

Artaxerxes had enjoyed all the stories and been blind to their significance; he was annoyed that Esther, a woman, his wife, had noticed it. Therefore he said testily:

"They were funny stories. Of course, being a woman you have no sense of humour . . ."

"But I said they were funny," Esther protested.

"Without appreciating them . . ." he retorted.

"I don't appreciate anything that diminishes my husband in my eyes."

"Oh," Artaxerxes' voice took on an edge, "you prefer the King to the man."

"I didn't say that, Artaxerxes. Don't twist the things I say, please."

"You are the one who twists things," he said angrily. "Everything that Haman says or does you twist into some kind of insult. He does a clever imitation, arranges an amusing charade, tells some very funny stories, and you say he is undermining my dignity. If that isn't the notion of a twisted mind I don't know what would be. Unless, like everybody else, you are jealous of Haman."

That was a ridiculous suggestion — and at the same time so dangerously near something like the truth that

116

Esther lost her temper and with it all sense of situation. She forgot that she was addressing the King of Persia and rapped out the sharp retort that she would have made if Uncle Mordecai had annoyed her.

"Jealous of that jumped-up little puppy with two rings on each finger and dirty fingernails, snuffling away with his Amalekitish accent. When I do anybody the honour of being jealous of him it'll be somebody different from Haman. All I hope is that when he decides — as he will decide, mark my words — to bite the hand that feeds him, you'll have enough sense left to draw it back in time."

Nobody, not his own mother, or his tutors, or even banished Vashti, had ever spoken to Artaxerxes like that. Still angry, and unable to think of an effective argument quickly, he took refuge in his dignity.

"I think you forget to whom you are speaking," he said pompously. "I am not in the habit of bandying words of abuse. I bid you good-night."

First thing in the morning he set on foot the arrangements for his banquet and pointedly omitted to invite Esther. Haman, of course, noticed the omission, and halfway through the feast improvised another charade, in one scene of which Zeresh, with her hair hastily arranged like Esther's, lay on a divan with a sulky expression on her face and refused all invitation to take part in the play. She was sick she said. The physicians were called and made careful examinations; nothing was wrong they said. Then finally one of them declared that he had tracked the trouble: the lady, he said, would never be able to leave her bed again, she was suffering from a grossly enlarged spleen. Since the spleen was the organ of the human body supposed to be responsible for the temper the implication was obvious and everybody saw the joke and laughed most heartily. When Esther was told about it she was very angry, because it showed plainly that Artaxerxes had either told Haman outright or dropped some very frank hints about the reason for her absence; and that smacked of grave disloyalty. So she tore up the letter of apology and explanation which she had spent a miserable evening writing while the feast was on, and decided that now Artaxerxes might make the first move towards a reconciliation.

This he actually did do a few days later when his temper had cooled; but he made the mistake of not coming to see her, but of sending an official with orders to ask after her health, which was, to do the King justice, a purely formal inquiry, part of the court etiquette. He had completely forgotten the charade, and if he had thought about it could not have guessed that Esther had heard about it. He was very shocked, therefore, to be told by the official that the Queen had sent back this answer: "Tell my Lord that my spleen is still increasing, but does not yet equal his own for size." And to do Esther justice, she had thought that the formal inquiry was just another piece of mockery.

That worsened the situation between them considerably. Both were proud, both were in love, and therefore very tender in their self-esteem, and neither would apologise. Haman, who had the Amalekitish inborn love of mischief for its own sake, fomented the quarrel for all he was worth. Artaxerxes, who was miserable in the secret places of his heart and missed the long interesting talks which had become part of his daily routine, turned to his favourite more and more. Haman had become a necessity to him, and they were now hardly ever apart. The favourite's conceit and mania for power reached demented proportions and one morning, when the quarrel between King and Queen had hardened down into what looked like permanent estrangement, Haman, meeting Mordecai at the gate and failing as usual to extract any sign of reverence, made up his mind that the stubborn old man should pay for his insolence with his life. The insults should be wiped out in blood. And now was the time.

CHAPTER
THIRTEEN

With all his faults, Haman was no fool. In itself, the removal of one old Jew presented no trouble at all. A hired assassin could do away with him very easily. A thug could wait at a corner or in a dark doorway and pull tight the lethal piece of cloth around his throat; a man with a dagger could knock at his door in the Street of Camels after dark and stab the man who opened it, without noise or fuss. There was only one thing which prevented such swift and simple action ... the old man's name. That name was inscribed upon the parchment now gathering dust with the record of Mirimah's rebellion; that name was even more indelibly inscribed somewhere in the King's mind. The parchment was dusty and the King was forgetful. But let the Jewish mourners once start about the streets crying that they bewailed the passing of Mordecai and some memory might stir. Artaxerxes took a curious, almost boyish interest in the queer customs of the varied races that owned his governorship in Shushan. There was a tiny colony of pottery-makers from Crete, who had a kiln and some huts at the end of the Street of Palms, and often on a morning ride he would stop and watch them at work, because their wheels were different from those of Persian potters, and they had a trick of working the colours into the clay instead of painting them on to the finished article. And the King's interest in Jewish mourning processions was quite notorious. It dated from the day when such a procession passed under the palace walls on its way to the Jewish cemetery just outside the town. The women were wailing and tearing their clothes that day for somebody named Zenoab — the name was spoken again and again in every accent of grief and bereavement. Artaxerxes had gone to the window and asked a bystander who was Zenoab, and in what way he had been so important. Zenoab, it was revealed, had been the humblest of the humble . . . an old man who removed refuse upon the back of his ancient donkey. But he was a Jew, and every Jew in Shushan had turned out for his funeral, and their wailing had drawn even the King to his window — and made him a little jealous. He had turned from the window and said to Haman, who was then a page:

"I am King of Persia, my boy, but when I go to my grave there'll be less fuss than there is about this dead donkey driver. Why do they tear their clothes?"

Haman, with his Amalekite's knowledge of Jewish history, had explained . . . and managed to make it sound very funny, so that the King had laughed. But although that was a long time ago, Artaxerxes had always been attracted by the sight and sound of a Jewish funeral; and he might lean out and hear the wailing for Mordecai and say: "But that was the man . . ." After that, if there had been obvious foul play,

121

the King would never rest until he had found out who was responsible for it.

There was, of course, the alternative of having the old man done away with and his body either thrown into the river or buried far out of the city. But that would constitute a "disappearance" and would be mentioned in the police report which Artaxerxes scanned, with varying degrees of attention, every morning before taking his ride. The compilation of the list of "Missing Persons" had been started many, many years previously as a protection for slave owners whose slaves had run away, but it had widened in scope, and each list now contained as many names of ordinary people as of slaves. Girls would run away with their lovers, wives would run away from their husbands, sons would run away with some of their father's property; and there were always a few people who had been murdered, or had lost their minds and wandered. If Mordecai just disappeared there was every chance that his name might appear in that list and Artaxerxes, reminded of the debt he owed him, would move heaven and earth until he was found — or avenged.

Thinking these matters over, Haman found himself remembering an old Arabian saying: "Where would a wise man hide a leaf? In a forest." And where would a dead man be better hidden than in a heap of dead men? Wipe out all Jews and Mordecai, anonymous and unmourned, is wiped out, too.

And Haman, avenged of Mordecai, is avenging Amalekite on all Israel — those pushing invaders who came out of Egypt and tried to grab all the best land. It

122

is a big scheme, a colossal scheme, but not too big for Haman, the second man in the Persian Empire. What is more, if he is clever, and he knows quite well that he is, he can turn this to his advantage, worm his way more firmly into favour, make an extra display of his loyalty.

Three evenings after he had decided upon his plan, after three days of waiting an apt opportunity, Haman was supping with the King, and everything was going merrily when a dish of artichokes was set on the table, each a little green island floating in a yellow sea of spiced and melted butter. They were the first of the season, and the King set to with a will. But Haman's appetite and his spirit seemed to have suffered a decline. He left his artichokes untasted and sat looking thoughtfully.

"Don't you like the dish?" asked Artaxerxes, plunging his buttery fingers into the rose-scented water and wiping them on the fringed napkin.

"Who? Me?" Haman asked, using one of his deliberately endearing little tricks of speech. There was no one else at the table.

"Yes, you. What's the matter with you?"

"An association of ideas. Jerusalem artichokes they call these. Jerusalem set me thinking about the Jews and that took away my appetite."

He pushed the plate from him, set his elbows on the table and his chin in his hands, and so sat, looking very solemn indeed.

"They had the most magnificent funeral to-day," Artaxerxes said, conversationally, helping himself to what artichokes remained in the dish. "I watched it for half an hour. They are very peculiar people."

"I suppose one could call the odour of an open sewer *peculiar* if one strained tolerance to the point of insanity. But revolting is a better word to use."

"Haman, Haman, we are supping," cried Artaxerxes. "I've noticed before that you were a little — shall we say prejudiced — against Jews. But surely that is no reason for losing your appetite and then trying to spoil mine by talking about open sewers."

Haman did not alter by the movement of a muscle the glowering expression of his face; but he directed his brooding stare at the King and said:

"You like my company because I make you laugh; and you have done me signal honour, for which I am most abjectly grateful. But I can't go on playing the fool for ever. I can laugh and joke, but I can also see as far into a brick wall as the next man, and at the risk of incurring your displeasure I am now asking your permission to speak seriously on one of the subjects that seems to me worth being serious about."

He had gained his first point, which was to arouse Artaxerxes' interest and curiosity.

"My dear Haman, since when had you been obliged to ask permission to speak on any subject?"

"Since the Jews were mentioned," Haman said. "They happen to be a subject concerning which your good sense fails you. You're like that unfortunate Lady of Tyremis who was given a lion cub for a pet, and never noticed how much it had grown until one day it

124

ate her for its noonday snack. Don't you remember the poem about it:

"She said it loved her. And in fact the old sinner
Said, 'I do love a lady between breakfast and
dinner.'"

"My dear Haman," Artaxerxes said again, "What are you talking about? Remember, I'm just a plain man; all this talk of open sewers and brick walls and lion cubs and poems is confusing my mind. Are you trying to be very tactful and tell me some bad news?"

"You could call it that," said Haman, deciding to come to the point. "You would agree, wouldn't you, that in a scattered, loosely-knit mixture of nationalities such as compose your empire, the most essential thing is to impose some sort of unity and overhead loyalty."

"And isn't that done? Isn't every decree I issue carried into every one of the provinces as fast as a horse can gallop, and posted and obeyed as though it were Shushan itself."

"To the outward eye. It might surprise you to know that no Jew pays your rules more than lip-service; that you have in every part of your empire a group of people who hate and despise you, and will go on doing so until they have brought you down. If you think they are a humble, harmless subject people you are at liberty of course to go on thinking that. But you think wrongly. Many are poor and engaged in humble trades, but many, many more are bankers and pawnbrokers and moneylenders; they hold a far greater proportion of the

125

wealth in the kingdom than any other single group, and far more than their numbers justify. And at any given moment they are likely to band together and say: 'Who is this Artaxerxes, merely a man; we Jews only obey Jehovah.' Jehovah is the name of their outlandish God and He speaks direct to men called prophets, who, of course, can tell the people that He has told them just what they want the people to believe. They do hold entertaining funerals . . . but they're very dangerous, and they have been responsible for at least one immensely important funeral." He paused dramatically.

"And that was?"

"The funeral of their own kingdom. David and Solomon had set that on firm and apparently unshakable foundations; nobody outside could have touched it if the Jews could have been loyal to their own King; but they couldn't. Solomon's son wasn't Jehovah-fearing enough for them, so they split up and made two silly little states, quite easily overcome; and even when they were fighting for their lives their prophets were foretelling disaster because the petty kings under whom they were fighting weren't holy enough.

"A people who can't obey even their own kings can't very well be expected to obey anybody else's. And to me it is an ominous sign that in almost every country which we have conquered lately the Jews had previously been favoured and protected, and in some cases shown honour."

"That was very true of Babylon," said Artaxerxes, thoughtfully, when Haman, who had been speaking vehemently, paused for breath.

126

"I am anxious that it shouldn't be true of Persia," Haman said. "I may be alone of your counsellors to hold this opinion but they are the worm in the bud, the thorn in the foot, the loose nail in the horseshoe that brings the whole thing down.

"I never regarded them of the slightest importance," said Artaxerxes.

"They count on that. Who cares or notices that they won't eat any save their own specially-prepared food; that they won't give even lip-service to the gods of the country in which they live; that they won't marry a person of another race; that on feast days their shops are open, but always closed on the Sabbath, as they call it. They have preserved themselves, an alien and potentially dangerous group in our very midst . . . and you think they have entertaining funerals."

"I will issue orders," said Artaxerxes. "I will send out special orders that on this Sabbath day every Jew shop is to be open and every Jew about his business. I will say that every Jew is to attend the next sacrifice in the groves of Astaroth. I will make them conform."

"Lots of people have tried that," Haman said, elaborately casual now that he had started Artaxerxes' rancour. "It is useless; they would die first."

"Then they must die," Artaxerxes said crossly.

"It would mean a massacre," said Haman craftily.

"Then it must be a massacre. Better a massacre than an enemy in our midst. Not that I like or approve of massacres — but they are necessary at times, as in the case of Mirimah."

"The Jews are a thousand times more dangerous than Mirimah ever was."

"Then they must be treated in the same way."

"It disgusts you, doesn't it?" Haman asked in a voice of sympathetic indulgence. "I always said that if you have one quality which is dangerous and unsuitable in your position, it is the quality of mercy. It is intensely endearing — if I may say so . . . but . . . Look, would you like to leave this entirely to me? Give me your seal and I'll attend to the orders and everything. You need have absolutely nothing to do with it. I saw the danger and I dealt with it in the only possible way. Leave it to me."

Something that was squeamish and sentimentalist in Artaxerxes had reared its head when he had spoken the word "massacre." It was with intense relief that he took the ring with the Great Seal from his finger and handed it over to Haman the Amalekite. Haman went out with the power of life and death in his hands.

CHAPTER
FOURTEEN

Mordecai still came regularly to the gate to gossip with his friend the porter and to gather the latest news of Esther. After a time he had heard, in a roundabout way, that there had been a quarrel; and once he had thought of writing to her to remind her that it was Artaxerxes who had chosen her, and to point out that it was a wife's duty to bear herself meekly before her husband. But he had thought better of that, for he knew his Esther, and knew that to a girl of her high spirit such advice might result in behaviour of the opposite kind; and, also, he trusted her. They had themselves had little quarrels, and if Esther were proved wrong she could apologise very sweetly, and if she were proved right she could accept an apology with grace, and in either case the reconciliation had been very sweet. Esther, Mordecai thought, and hoped, might know what she was doing better than he could. So he did not write.

But the morning came when he found his friend the porter absent from his familiar place; the new man said that he was ill; and Mordecai went across to the little house where he and the porter and Corin had once drunk wine together, to inquire after him. The porter did not look very pleased to see him, nor, though his face was paler than usual and his manner very strange, did he seem ill enough to warrant absence from duty. He appeared to be packing with some haste and muddle.

"Yes, I'm ill," he said, in answer to Mordecai's inquiry. "I'm going into the country for my health."

"To Corin's place," Mordecai asked innocently, for Corin, when his master Bigthana was hanged, had borrowed some money and started a small silk farm.

"Yes, to Corin's place," said the porter with such obvious relief that Mordecai wondered.

"And you don't intend to come back, you are retiring?" he asked, eyeing the bundles.

"My health . . ." said the porter, wrapping some rugs into a bundle. "Uncertain health makes uncertain plans."

"Well, I shall miss you very much," Mordecai said. "I'm not just saying that, I shall miss you. And I shall pray God that your health may improve and that your retirement may be long and happy."

The porter dropped the rugs and looked stricken.

"You are one of us . . ." he said in a broken voice. "Listen . . . sit down. I ordered the mule for ten o'clock, there's just time to tell you. But you must promise not to repeat what I tell you or there'll be a panic, and that wouldn't help at all." Mordecai sat down on the bed, which had been stripped, and waited. "Nobody knows that I am a Jew . . . at least, nobody ever bothered to ask and I didn't tell them; it wasn't wise, you agree? So they didn't bother to keep the news from me. Astus the scribe whispered it about . . .

130

there's going to be a massacre. Haman ordered it last evening. The decrees are being written out at this moment, and are going out, and when the last courier reaches the last outpost the sign will be given and the orders will go up everywhere at once. Every Jew in Persia is going to be killed. I'm clearing out. I shall go to Corin and tell him and we'll leave together. And now I'm telling you. Maybe you'd better come with us."

"Where to," Mordecai asked, as soon as he had recovered his breath and his capacity for speech. "You know how far the Persian laws run, don't you? From India to Ethiopia. Can you and Corin get away from that?"

"We can only try," said the porter. "Corin had a wife . . . not a Jew; she's Phoenician, and he always kept on good terms with her family even after she was dead. And I think that if we could get to Tyre, or Sidon, they'd put us on a ship. We can but try it. And you might as well come with us. Run now and put a few things — a few things, mark you — into a little bundle and I'll make room for it on my mule. Only hurry."

"That is a most generous offer," said Mordecai, "and I do appreciate it. I can't accept it, however. If what you say is true . . ."

"As God is in heaven, it *is* true," said the porter. "Here, see for yourself. I went into the scribes' room when I saw them go to breakfast and stole a copy. I wanted it for Corin. Me being such an ignorant fellow and him a bit of a scholar, I thought he could read it in case he didn't believe me. I don't think he would, he always thought so well of the King. But there it is, you can read for yourself."

Mordecai stood and read the decree that doomed every member of his race within the bounds of Persia.

"May I keep this, please?" he asked.

"No. Oh no. I tell you I stole it for Corin. If I just went to him with a story he'd say I was raving or hysterical or something. I must have it for proof."

"Then may I take a copy?"

"What for," asked the porter suspiciously. "To start a panic and set the thing moving before I have time to get away I suppose. Give it back . . ."

"There is one person, just one person," said Mordecai solemnly, "who might be able to help if I could prove my story; but this person will be even more difficult to persuade than your cousin Corin, because this person is also an admirer of the King's. It is Corin's belief balanced against this person's; one can save Corin's skin, perhaps, the other might save us all. Let me at least take a copy."

"If you *vow* to show it only to this one person — though who he can be I can't imagine," said the porter weakening. "But a vow, mind."

"I vow," said Mordecai gravely, "not to speak of this matter nor to show my copy to any save the one person in whom all our hopes rest. And if our blood does not run in all the streets in all the cities of Persia it will be due, in measure, to this one person, and also, in large measure, to you."

"May God so ordain," said the porter piously. "Take your copy, then, before my mule arrives."

132

Mordecai drew out the writing materials which he always carried, thanking God as he did so, that he did carry them in case some illiterate person requested him to write a letter. Once his hand set to work it grew steady, and he wrote as calmly and composedly as though he had been in his own room. But some small fragment of his mind was working upon another line of thought. His writing was very characteristic and recognisable, and his copy would not, like the porter's filched one, bear the King's seal. So when it was made he folded them both into the same shape and gave the porter the copy, which he stuffed away without inspecting it. The original copy he placed in the wallet at his girdle. It was duplicity — it was cheating; but the lives of many mattered more than one man's, and if Corin couldn't accept the evidence of his cousin's arrival and of the unsealed copy of the decree, then that was Corin's affair. Anyway, Mordecai thought, I am trying to save them too; because before they reach Tyre and safety the couriers will have reached the outposts and the decree will be posted. Swift horses — slow mule; and Corin will want to pack a lot of rubbish, too. If we are saved, they will be saved; if we are lost, they are lost with us. I must do the best I can for us all — God help me.

At that moment the mule which the porter had ordered came clattering to the door, and the refugee began to load the more precious of his possessions on to its back. Mordecai, remembering how the man had offered to share the mule with him, and remembering, too, all the other matters for which he had reason to be grateful to him, helped with the loading and then bade him a grave, affectionate farewell. He wished him safe travelling and a happy arrival. The porter, who seemed overcome by terror and urgency now that he was in the open street and on the point of departure, could hardly reply. He seized the mule's bridle and began to pull it forward. Then he remembered and called back over his shoulder. "I hope your business goes well, too, my brother." Then he hurried away, out of the city of Shushan and out of the life of Mordecai, who hurried away in the other direction, to reach his little house on the Street of Camels, where he sat down to write to Esther.

CHAPTER
FIFTEEN

Esther read the letter with feelings of horror and terror and dismay. The decree — signed by Haman using Artaxerxes' seal ring, but she did not know that — fell out of the package, complete proof, if proof were needed, that Mordecai had not appealed to her without reason. His own letter explained the situation baldly and briefly, and told her that now was the moment to reveal her nationality and ask the King's protection for *her* people.

A gust of something very like hysteria shook her; she could have laughed and cried together to think how very simple her orders sounded and how impossible they were to carry out. She and Artaxerxes were estranged; they had not seen nor spoken to one another for a whole month; and with that stupid quarrel still festering between them, with no word of apology offered on either side, here was Uncle Mordecai writing that this was the moment when she should go to her husband and say, "Please save the Jews because I am a Jewess myself." What a way of making peace with him.

She saw, with a horribly sharpened vision, every detail of that planned massacre . . . the horror of blood, the broken bones, the screaming women smitten down, the men cut off in their prime . . . the little children utterly guiltless of anything save their parentage . . . all terrified and then, at last, all dead. And she saw, too, the full extent, the full, appalling extent of Mordecai's trust and hope in her. It was against just such a day as this that he had forced her into being Queen. And she had failed him. She saw the horrible extent and the reason for her failure. She had fallen in love with Artaxerxes. If she had kept her head and her heart she would not have cared about Haman making fun of him; would not have noticed Haman at all. She had betrayed every Jew in Persia, all those men and women and children. By falling in love and being outspoken. She should have remembered why she was offered for selection and why she was chosen; she should have been tactful and gracious and pleasing, but never in love. That way she might have kept her influence over her husband and had something to use now. As it was she was helpless. It seemed to her to be most important that Mordecai should know just how helpless she was; she couldn't bear to think of him trusting her. Not for one more wasted moment must he go on trusting her. She sat down with tears of remorse and sorrow still damp on her cheeks and wrote him a letter as blunt and brief as his own, telling him that she was helpless. She had, she said, offended the King. She wasted no time in explaining how the quarrel had arisen, or in trying to excuse herself. She had offended him and he was still angry with her, and it was thirty days since they had spoken to, or seen, one another. Court etiquette forbade that she should force herself into his presence, and if she tried to apologise now and then asked him a favour, it would be all too obvious, and he would become angrier than ever.

She delivered this letter to Hatach, who had taken the place of Hegai, and impressed him with the importance of having it immediately delivered. But Hatach, having seen the superscription and the humble address, imagined that Her Majesty was merely ordering a new pair of shoes from some old Jewish cobbler. Women always imagined that their small affairs were of the utmost importance, he had found. So he did not bother about the prompt delivery and Mordecai, who had spent the intervening time thinking and hoping that Esther had already begun to obey the orders he had given her, was immensely disappointed and grievously displeased to read her confession of helplessness. He kept the messenger waiting while he sat down and wrote to her exactly the words he would have spoken if he had been given a chance to get near her.

"Your communication, my dear Esther, has shocked and astonished me. You may imagine that you have reached a position where you are above racial discrimination, but I venture to tell you that it is not so. When the Jews perish, you perish with them. I explained to you, when I persuaded you to become a candidate for the crown, that an evil day was approaching, and I was confident, perhaps foolishly confident, that in *you* all our race had a champion who would fight for us in that evil day. The time is now. I told you then that God worked through His tools, and that they could be good or bad; the good were cherished, the bad destroyed. Perhaps you can recall that conversation. You were made Queen of Persia in order that you might in this crisis be Jehovah's tool for our salvation. If you prove to be a bad tool you will be destroyed and God will choose another to save us. Do you now choose between good and evil and remember that there is no half-measure. We are one people; with us you stand or fall. And for you, with your special privilege, there is a special judgment, for if you fail us, you also fail God."

The sweat shone on his brow and his hands were shaking as he sealed that letter and gave it into the messenger's hand. "It is the most urgent and important letter that you have carried. See that it is delivery safely and promptly," he said. He would have given the boy a coin, but he remembered that he had nothing, not even a penny, having been too distraught since the porter's departure to think about earning money. So the boy, who thought with Hatach that the Queen's business with this old man must be of the most trivial nature, and who had gained nothing by his errand, did not hasten to deliver the letter, and Hatach was equally dilatory. Esther suffered in this crisis from her reputation for being reasonable and kind; a fiercer Queen, more given to easy anger and ferocious punishment, would have been better served. When Esther received Mordecai's letter the span of days which the porter had mentioned had already run, and all over the empire the notices were being posted. On the thirteenth day of the twelfth month — a general massacre of the Jews was ordered.

Esther read her doom in a letter from a kinsman; the ordinary Jews read it, or heard it read from notices posted in public places in the cities and towns and villages on one hundred and twenty-seven provinces. But the running backwards of the blood, the stopping of the breath, was the same in the gilded marble palace and in the dusty market place. And for Esther it was worse. The ordinary Jew was doomed to suffering, to terror, to death; but he was not responsible either for his own fate or for those of his fellows. Esther had the weight of all this doom to bear.

Because I fell in love with him, she thought, and so minded what he did and what was done to him. But Jehovah, and Mordecai, and Artaxerxes had not been mistaken in Esther. She was no sawdust stuffed figure with a pretty face. This time she neither trembled nor cried. She hastily scribbled a message to Mordecai: "You gather the Jews together and pray," it read, "I will act. And if I die, I die."

And while every Jew within the bounds of that wide empire, too vast to escape from, too well organised to offer any refuge, was facing death — with all its accompanying horrors within a few days, wailing, praying, tearing their clothes, conscious of their helplessness, Esther the Queen, who was one of them, and who knew that death in a most peculiar form might strike her within a matter of minutes, sat down at her dressing table before her silver mirror, called to her slaves for attendance, and began carefully to make up her face.

CHAPTER
SIXTEEN

After all that time of waiting, while Artaxerxes sampled the beauty and the company of many other women, had not been wasted. Esther, straight from the Street of Camels, from her cloistered, academic life, had known little of the ways by which women enhanced their beauty. In that year of waiting she had, almost against her will, learned a great deal. And this morning, at a moment when every other woman of her race was tearing her poor garments or her rich clothes to tatters and putting ashes on her head in every province between Ethiopia and India, Esther in the heart of the palace that was the heart of Shushan that was the heart of the empire, was putting into use every fragment of knowledge that she had ever gained about the subject of beauty.

Her women were full of amazement. Why make oneself so beautiful in the morning when the King could not possibly be expected until evening? And when — they counted on their fingers — thirty evenings had already passed without a visit or an invitation. Her Majesty was a strange woman. And when, looking amazingly and unusually beautiful, Esther finally said, "That will do," and stood up as though to leave, one of them, bolder than the rest, asked:

"My lady, where do you go at this hour?"

"I am going to seek an audience of the King," Esther said simply.

"But . . . but . . ." the woman stammered, "the King is in his council chamber. My lady . . . this position had never arisen before . . . but you do *know* the rule? Only those who have appointments are admitted. Anyone, no matter whom, who tries to burst in . . . my lady, they kill him. It is a silly rule . . . but suppose it so happened that they didn't make an exception in your case . . ."

There were, she thought, plenty of nobles whose daughters, sisters, nieces, had wanted to be Queen who would be only too glad to force the silly law to its limit in this case. If her Majesty, without invitation or appointment, forced an entry during council hours — well, there was the law . . . no one could argue against that. And the late Queen had come to grief through obeying the laws, if the stories could be believed; this one was going dead against them, and silly as they might sound to any reasonable person they were laws and not lightly to be disregarded.

"I know," Esther said. "I haven't an invitation or an appointment and unless my husband holds out his gold sceptre as a sign that I am forgiven for intruding . . . then the law is broken and anything might happen to me. But I have to speak with him upon a matter of importance, and I must take the risk."

"But, my lady . . . the council hours will end some time."

"Yes, and without my knowledge the King will be gone out hunting. I think I can take the risk." She put on the look of a petted, pampered favourite, one who might dare anything. But the woman who had counted those thirty days on her fingers, caught her breath and vowed a brace of doves to the goddess Astaroth if nothing unfortunate happened.

And so Esther set out across the garden for the main palace where the audience chamber stood. He might, she thought, take this opportunity of getting rid of her. After all, she had annoyed him and spoken frankly and proudly. He had only to sit quite still when she forced her way into his presence and the guards would strike. Oh, if only she had sent that letter of apology which she had written, not torn it up in annoyance at hearing that she had been mimicked at the feast. What an evil thing pride was . . . and yet what a good thing . . . for it was pride that was strengthening her now; pride held her head up and kept her limbs steady. Pride made her say: If I die, I die . . . and pray God I die calmly without making a spectacle of myself.

And it was pride that enabled her to brush the guards aside and to step into the audience chamber, which might easily become a slaughter-house, with a step unhurried and assured.

Oddly enough, as soon as she had made her forced entry, pride deserted her. She had come here on a special errand, an errand that she had risked her life to perform. But at the moment when the guards fell back and the whole council chamber lay before her, her sense of doom, and of destiny and of daring, fell away.

Artaxerxes sat at the end of the room on a little platform. The great throne, with its jewelled peacock framework, was not used on ordinary occasions, and he sat in a simple gold chair whose arm-rests were lions' heads. And he wore a simple white linen gown embroidered in scarlet and a circlet of gold, set with rubies, on his head. The sun shone through the pillars and touched his left check and shoulder. He looked very young and very bored, and then the disturbance at the doorway drew his attention and although he still looked very young he also looked very stern and stately and very un-bored. And the thing which lately, through day and night, Esther had so heartily regretted — that she loved him — came uppermost, and he ceased, for a moment, to be the Great King who held life and death in his hands, the Mighty One whose presence one entered uninvited under pain of death, and was just the man whom she loved, with whom she had jokes, and long conversations, and silly little quarrels.

She was looking at him, not with fear and respect, but with simple admiration and love when he looked at her. For a second he sat motionless and then, fumbling for the gold sceptre which was always laid beside him, but which was never needed because nowadays nobody dared force themselves into the council chamber, he held it out, plain, in the sight of all the assembly. He was, for all his appearance of youth and his occasional immaturities of mind, a man of great experience with women, and he recognised the look of love on Esther's face. But she was, after all, the one who had started the quarrel, and he mustn't make things too easy for her.

143

So having saved her life by holding out the sceptre, he addressed her very formally and said:

"Queen Esther, you have some request to make of me?"

Until that moment she had not given the form of her request a thought. Mordecai's letter had shattered her, and her one aim had been to make her peace with the King and talk to him. But as she looked round at the courtiers and the other petitioners, formal, abject, amused or annoyed by the interruption of her arrival, she knew that this was not the moment for making a direct appeal. A feminine instinct which she had never known she possessed took charge, and she said in a very lighthearted, indeed flippant, manner: "Yes, my Lord, I have a great favour to ask of you. If it please you, will you and the Lord Haman come to a banquet in my apartments this evening?"

Ha, ha, Artaxerxes thought, pleased and triumphant. "Leave them alone and they'll come home," as the old rhyme has it. She's come to her senses. Me *and* Haman. That is good. It foretells peace between my wife and my favourite, and that is all I asked.

Aloud he said: "I am very pleased to accept your invitation, Queen Esther; and I can answer for the Lord Haman also."

"I shall then prepare and anticipate for the banquet with great pleasure," Esther said, equally formally, and withdrew. The business of the audience chamber resumed its course and the Queen of Persia, who had once earned part of the family income by superintending the preparation of banquets in better-class

144

households, went into the kitchen quarters of the Palace of Shushan and for an hour harried the cooks with advice and reproof. A less honest woman might have been ashamed to admit that she knew anything about the preparation of vegetables, the making of sauces; a more modest woman might have left the choice of wines to her butler, but Esther was determined that this should be a feast to outshine all feasts, and she gave it the whole of her attention.

She reaped her reward when Artaxerxes leaned back, replete, and said seriously that it was the best meal he had ever eaten.

"It's put me into such excellent humour that if you asked me at this moment for the half of my kingdom it should be yours," he said, half-seriously, half-teasingly. And Esther thought . . . is this the moment? She never knew what it was that held her back at that point from asking the one favour she craved — the order to cancel the massacre. Something did. As clearly as though a bell had sounded in her mind rang the thought that the time was not yet. Something remained to be done. She had no idea what it was. But a good tool was obedient, yielding to the master's hand — and the time was not yet; of that she was certain. So, adhering to that light and flippant manner which had come upon her as a sickness might come, she said:

"All I have to ask, my Lord, is that this pleasant company might gather together again to-morrow. That will only cost two hours of your time . . . Am I wrong in thinking that that is of less value than half your kingdom, or do I ask too much?" And amidst the laughter a discussion arose as to whether one's time or one's possessions were more valuable. And all the time Esther was watching Haman, trying to find out the secret of why the King valued him so much that he would quarrel, even with her, on his behalf. And all at once she knew exactly what it was. Haman was unexpected; his wit, his sulkiness, even the extravagance of his flattery were unlike anyone's because they had that quality of unexpectedness. She realised suddenly that the thing from which Artaxerxes suffered was boredom; for everything there was a rule, and a pattern, and without knowing it the King set an enormous value on anything that broke the rules and altered the pattern. He had married her because she hadn't plastered her face with paint, hadn't smelt of musk, hadn't tried to please him. She had broken that pattern. And although later on she had broken another set of rules by speaking to him so frankly, he hadn't resented the rudeness, only the criticism of Haman, who broke all the rules even more vigorously. A great, heady sense of power came to her with that thought — if I could just disillusion him about Haman I could replace him. Then there would be no wound. To-morrow, when I plead for the Jews and strike at Haman I must do so in some dramatic, unusual manner, not just make the accusation and the plea. I must do it in some such manner that even though Artaxerxes is disturbed he is also entertained. From that moment until Artaxerxes and Haman took their leave of her she watched the favourite closely. And when at last the curtains closed behind them she thought, *if* I succeed to-morrow, if I manage to destroy Haman, he need not be missed. In future I can be both Esther and Haman to Artaxerxes.

Artaxerxes left the Queen's apartments a little sulkily. A man, any man, had the right to stay with his wife and to make up a quarrel in a proper fashion. But during the last month Haman had taken advantage of the quarrel and tried to make Esther appear as a slightly ridiculous schoolmarmish figure; so when it grew late and Haman showed no signs of intending to leave them alone together Artaxerxes had himself risen and come away, accompanied by Haman. There was something weak and silly about that which the King regretted. He was sorry that he had ever taken Haman into his confidence about the quarrel; Haman had been anything but tactful. To do him justice — and on the whole Artaxerxes liked to act and to think justly — Haman didn't realise that he loved Esther, and that the quarrel had given him considerable pain. Haman had just thought that it was a stupid quarrel between two people who didn't much care for one another and had tried to holster up the King's self-esteem by making the Queen look ridiculous. But to-morrow evening he would make it quite clear that he *did* love his wife, and that the quarrel was ended and no more jokes or witty remarks at her expense would be acceptable.

Haman, going home to his brand new palace to his wife, walked on air. The Queen, haughty baggage as she was, had been obliged to give in to him. By asking him to her feast to-night and again to-morrow she had recognised that the King could not be happy without him, even with her. Esther was, he admitted, a danger;

she was nearly as witty and unexpected as he was himself. If this most fortunate quarrel hadn't arisen between them Haman's position might have been threatened. It wasn't often that a favourite had much to fear from a woman; women were generally stupid and bad company. But he had been threatened by Esther . . . they had fought out their unannounced little war and he had won. She had been forced to accept him.

In the midst of this self-congratulatory mood the uncomfortable memory of something that happened that afternoon, struck him. And as he was telling Zeresh about the very successful banquet he spoke of that memory. "I have beaten her at her own game," he said. "They quarrelled, and for thirty days she has been left alone. Now she asks us both, to-night and again to-morrow. That is a triumph . . . but do you know, that squalid old Jew was in the gateway again, staring straight through me, greasy cap on his head and head unbowed. It makes me so angry."

"But why?" asked Zeresh, wishing that he would stop chattering and get into bed so that she could return to sleep. Bad enough that he should go to the Queen's feast without her — and be asked again for to-morrow, without being wakened and kept awake to talk about Jews: "You're going to have your revenge on *all* Jews, aren't you, darling? For this special one who won't make his bow, I'd make a special gallows, twice as high as usual, and hang him first so that all the rest can see."

"That is a wonderful idea," Haman said, "I'll have the gallows built to-morrow."

He fell asleep, blissfully happy, thinking of his revenge upon Mordecai . . . horrible, squalid, disrespectful old Jew, Mordecai. Mordecai doomed to extinction with the rest of his race, dead leaf buried amongst dead leaves . . . never be insulting again. Mordecai.

The name which sounded soothingly in Haman's ears as he fell asleep presently rang with the rousing note of a trumpet call in the wakeful ear of his master. For Artaxerxes, King of Persia, was suffering, for the first time in his life, from insomnia. He had come from the Queen's apartments and been made ready for his bed. He had thought for a time about Esther and Haman and his behaviour to them both to-morrow; and that being settled he had tried to sleep. But the thought of Haman had intruded itself and had passed, by a natural process of association to the thought of the massacre of the Jews; and there all sleep had deserted the King. The idea of massacre repelled him. Haman had made it sound very necessary, made it sound like shrewd statesmanship, but what it boiled down to in the end was a lot of dead bodies — men, women, and children, just people who had been alive and were suddenly dead. Not a nice thought, reflected Artaxerxes, turning to his other side and desperately seeking sleep.

Haman said the Jews were dangerous, and for a moment Artaxerxes had believed him . . . believed him long enough to give him permission to exterminate them and lend him that seal ring which the little demon hadn't remembered to give him back. Must ask for it in the morning. In the morning . . . easy to plan when one knew there would be a morning ... presently there would be a lot of people for whom there would be no morning ... imagine, no morning, no awakening, no more going to bed, no more eating, no more laughing, no more plans of any sort.

I'm going mad, the King thought, seeking a cool place on a pillow that seemed stuffed with lumps of burning charcoal. And this is mere discomfort, said a voice in his mind ... How does that compare with actual *pain*, being stabbed, or beheaded or hanged or smothered?

By all the gods! thought Artaxerxes, and sat up and clapped his hands.

The slave on duty outside the door came running to know if his master needed water, wine, fruit juice, food ... would like another cover or a cover removed, would like the window more open, more closed, would like to be fanned.

"Can you play the harp? The lute? The dulcimer?"

"No, my Lord. No, my Lord. No, my Lord. I have no skill at all, my Lord."

"What can you do, fool?"

"I can play chess, my Lord."

"But to play with you I must sit up, and I want to lie down and gradually go to sleep."

"I could ... I could read to you, my Lord," said the slave, nervous but eager.

"That might serve," said Artaxerxes. "Take a lamp and go to the records room. Don't bring the first thing that comes to hand, they're the ordinary records that we deal with every day. Bring something long ago and far away, something out of the ordinary."

The slave, who knew how slaves did their work unless strictly supervised, ran away determined to bring something that had been put into a corner and was dusty and cobwebbed. Holding the lamp high he looked around the records room where the scrolls lay, neat and tidy in their racks. Then he looked higher and saw some disused ones heaped haphazardly upon the tops of the cupboards. He dragged up a stool and standing on it reached down the first scroll that his hand touched. Jumping down and holding it to the light he saw that it was thickly covered with dust and sealed at the edges with cobwebs. Certainly an old one. He brushed it and read the label on its outside. "An Account of a Most Fortunate Escape," he read. That sounded promising; just what he was looking for. He hurried back to the King's bedchamber, set the lamp so that the light fell upon the scroll but not upon the bed, untied the tape and unrolled the first ten inches of the parchment.

The scribe, although he had written that record on the morning after the happening it reported, had imagined himself writing for posterity and had used the historical style.

"Now in the twelfth month of the seventh year of the reign of Artaxerxes, King of Persia and Lord of all lands between . . ." the slave began to read and then faltered into silence.

"I thought I told you to find an old story," said Artaxerxes peevishly.

"My Lord, I thought I had done so. My Lord, this was not with the ordinary records, I swear. It was high on a cupboard, tossed away, covered with dust and spider's webs."

"How could it be? It is a contemporary document. They are all kept together. You lazy swine, you snatched up the first thing that came to hand. You shall be beaten for this!"

"My Lord, indeed I took it from a cupboard top; I climbed on a stool to search amongst the old scrolls. See — the marks of the dust which I brushed away, and see here — a cobweb I failed to remove. My Lord, I beg of you . . ."

It was true enough, the scroll was not in the condition one would expect if it had been taken from the ordinary rack.

"I will return it at once, my Lord, and fetch another."

"No, wait. I would like to know *why* this scroll was set aside from the others. Read on a little. Unless it is a duplicate of one on the racks and thus of no value, I shall sharply rebuke the chief scribe in the morning. Read on."

". . . between Ethiopia and India, Protector of the Poor, Giver of Justice, Great . . ."

"Pass that over, we know all that," said Artaxerxes impatiently.

"Then did two lords who stood near the King's person most evilly and foully plot and conspire against his safety and well-being, their names being Bigthana and Teresh . . ."

152

"Ah," said Artaxerxes softly, and settled himself to listen. The slave read well, he had a beautiful voice and, once he had got over his nervousness, gave the story its full dramatic value. He read of the gazelle hunt and the trial and the execution. And finally, slowing his voice before the end, read: "'Thus was the evil intent of traitors confounded through the loyalty of Mordecai, a Jew from the Street of Camels.' That is the end, my Lord," said the slave, and began to reroll the scroll.

"Mordecai, a Jew," said Artaxerxes, slowly and thoughtfully. "Boy, go back to the record room and look in the rack labelled 'Honours and Awards in the Present Reign.' If I remember rightly it stands third on the left of the door; but it is plainly labelled and the records are arranged in the order of their year. Bring me the record of the seventh and the eighth year. Hurry."

When the slave returned the King said: "Now hold the lamp for me," and with his own hands he unrolled the records. There was no mention of Mordecai's name at the end of the seventh year's honours, but the thing had happened in the twelfth month, perhaps there had not been time. But the record of the eighth year was equally void of any mention of honour or award done to Mordecai. In fact no Jew was mentioned at all.

"I owed him my life, and I gave him nothing," said Artaxerxes, in a stunned voice. "How could I be so ungrateful, or forgetful?"

"This scroll, which might have reminded you, my Lord, was set aside," said the slave, trying to please his master by offering him an excuse.

"That is true. All the same . . . here is a pension for life given because a fellow pleased me with his harp-playing, and a title conferred on a forester who gave me a good day's sport. But for the man who saved my life . . . nothing. That is regrettable, but it can be remedied. Very well, put out the lamp and leave me now."

He settled down to sleep planning a joke on Haman. Haman was so fond of playing jokes himself, but he never had thought of one so rich as this. In the morning he would say to Haman . . . Smiling, like a schoolboy who has planned a prank, the King of Persia fell asleep at last.

CHAPTER
SEVENTEEN

"The morning's greetings, Haman," said Artaxerxes.

"The morning's greetings, my Lord. It is a beautiful morning."

"A very beautiful morning."

They looked at one another. Haman thought that the King looked lively and a little amused as though he knew a pleasing secret.

"I have been waiting for you, Haman. I need your advice. Suppose — that is just supposing, you know — but suppose there were a man whom I wanted to honour more than anybody had ever been honoured before in the history of the world. What could I do? Pensions and titles are very ordinary, aren't they? What could I do to show the most special, the most intense honour?"

With no little difficulty Haman prevented the pleasure he felt from showing itself upon his face. Whom but himself could the King wish to honour; nothing had happened, no new favourite had arisen; it could only be himself.

He pretended to think deeply and then be visited by inspiration.

"As you say, pensions and titles are ordinary, especially now, since you are so generous — why only last evening, if you remember, you offered half your kingdom as a reward for a pleasant banquet. Such generosity makes it a little difficult when it comes to the question of *really* wanting to show somebody honour. In fact, I'm afraid there's only one thing that you could do." He laughed as though he had thought of something amusing.

"And that is?" Artaxerxes asked, watching him more closely than he realised.

"Give him your royal robes, lend him your crown, set him on your own horse, and let him ride through the streets of Shushan with a herald going ahead of him proclaiming that he was the man whom you took delight in honouring," said Haman, keeping his voice light. But the glitter of delightful anticipation shone in his eyes, and Artaxerxes thought shrewdly — so that's what Haman really wants; he is now speaking his dream. To be King for a day is his ambition — but would it end with the day?

The joke had lost its humour. He had imagined that Haman would suggest the bestowal of an estate or a gift of money; then the joke would have been to make the gift to Mordecai first and then later, perhaps this evening, to make exactly the same gift to Haman. But now . . .

"I think that is a delightful suggestion," said Artaxerxes gravely. "And since you had the wit to think of it, Haman, you shall have the honour of carrying it out. There is a man whom I intend to honour, and I

156

want everything done that you have suggested — the robes, the crown, the horse and the proclamation. You understand, everything, just as you said."

"But you must first tell, my Lord, the name of this so-fortunate man whom you would honour."

"Oh yes, of course," said Artaxerxes. "His name is Mordecai; he is a Jew and he lives on the Street of Camels."

There was a moment of complete silence.

"Everyone, even I, forgot him," Artaxerxes said, "but he did save my life, and every *loyal* subject will gladly join me in honouring him."

"Most certainly," said Haman, dry-lipped. "Every loyal subject . . ."

"I'll leave all the arrangements to you, Haman. You still have my seal? Good. Then you can act for me. I'll see you this evening at the Queen's apartments."

Never, never in the whole history of the world, Haman thought as he staggered away, had anything so bitter, so horrible, happened to any man. To have planned an honour for oneself and then been ordered to bestow it upon a loathsome, insolent, most hated enemy. At this very moment the workmen were rearing that specially high gallows; presently they would stop work to stare at Mordecai riding past wearing the King's clothes and the King's crown; they would listen to the herald's announcement . . . it just wasn't bearable.

But the orders of the King must be obeyed, and Haman obeyed them. Mordecai, grave, unmoved, regarding all this curious procedure as part of Jehovah's inscrutable design, rode around the streets of the city. He passed, at certain points, the posters which announced the ordering and the date of the massacre; he passed at one point a place where men were hammering a new gallows together; he passed everywhere little groups of people of his own race wearing the sackcloth of sorrow and the ashes of mourning. They looked at him, bewildered by the strange sight of a Jew being honoured at such a time, and in some of their hearts there was a hope they dared not admit.

Haman, having arranged the procession of honour, retired to his own house and sulked there. He tried to unburden himself to Zeresh, who failed him in his hour of need and expressed the opinion that since Mordecai was a Jew and Haman had declared war on the Jews, he was likely to be more annoyed and depressed before long. The remark was shrewd, and one of the things Haman had admired about Zeresh was her shrewdness, her capacity for making unsentimental remarks; at this moment he found little comfort in it. He was still sulking, brooding over his grievance, tasting the bitterness of the first rebuff he had experienced in the whole of his meteoric career, when the chamberlain arrived to remind him that the Queen's banquet was about to begin. At that he rose hastily, donned his finest robe and all his jewels, and set out, desperately determined to regain the ground he felt he had lost: he would be witty, he would be gay, he would indulge in the most extravagant and, at the same time, subtle flattery. He must win back the King's favour.

Before Esther's feast had lasted ten minutes Haman was wondering why he had imagined that Artaxerxes was displeased with him. Nothing had changed. It was just like last evening. The food and the wine were exquisite; the King in high good humour; the Queen looked brilliantly beautiful, and was both easy to amuse and extremely amusing. Haman decided that he had been a fool to take Mordecai's honour as an insult to himself — after all, Artaxerxes hadn't known that Mordecai was his special enemy, he had merely wanted to do honour, belatedly, to the man who had saved his life. And Mordecai would not have long to enjoy his promotion; in the general massacre it would be easy to see to it that he was killed. Everything was all right, Haman thought, and set himself out to be amusing. And Esther, watching him, carried out the plan upon which she had determined. She revealed a hitherto unsuspected talent for mimicry, kinder than Haman's but no less funny; she capped his wildest flights of fancy, she replied to every one of his funny stories with a funny story of her own. Artaxerxes, who asked nothing better than that the company in which he found himself should be congenial and entertaining, enjoyed himself thoroughly, and at last, turning to Esther, said: "Last night I told you that half my kingdom was yours for the asking, and you asked only that I should come and enjoy myself here to-night. Now, if I repeat my offer, will you repeat your invitation?"

This was the moment.

"No, my Lord. I shall give no more feasts . . ." her voice, suddenly sombre, banished the gaiety. "You see, my Lord, I am going to die!"

There, even Haman could never have equalled that for unexpectedness and melodramatic utterance.

"Die?" Artaxerxes repeated, half rising and taking her by the shoulder. "What do you mean? Are you ill . . . have the physicians . . .?" Some secret, deadly disease, he thought, borne in brave silence . . . he thought of the quarrel, the month during which they had not spoken, and the bitter anguish of despair and remorse, a physical thing which could be tasted in the mouth, rose within him. "Esther," he breathed.

"No, I am in perfect health, but I have been sentenced to death, together with thousands of others of your subjects."

"Sentenced to death . . . Esther, you're joking," he faltered, thinking that, even for a joke, even at a feast, this was carrying things a *little* far.

"Do I look as though I were joking? Death is no matter for jesting, my Lord. No, the decree has gone out; I and all my race have been sentenced to death by our old enemy."

"Decree? What are you babbling about? Old enemy — who can be the enemy of the Queen of Persia? Who, in the name of madness, has the power to sentence *my wife* to death?"

Esther raised one hand. It was a beautiful hand, white and slender, tipped with henna, sparkling with jewels. It pointed across the table.

"There he sits," she said simply.

160

Artaxerxes stared stupidly at Haman and Haman stared stupidly back; his mouth opened and closed and opened and closed, but no sound emerged. Suddenly Artaxerxes felt as though he were strangling; he struggled to his feet and hurried out through the curtained archway into the garden. Anyone observing him might have imagined that he was escaping from a threatened danger, he walked so fast, seemed so intent upon putting a distance between himself and that lighted room. Three thoughts beat like a hammer in his head — Esther, whom he loved, was Jewish; all Jews were doomed to death: Haman had arranged it. Under each blow of the hammer his brain shuddered.

Within doors, across the glittering table, the glittering favourite faced the glittering Queen. Haman's face, even to the lips, was grey, and the sweat of terror stood on his brow. Presently the grey lips moved.

"I did not know," he said, "believe me, I did not know. I meant you no harm."

"No. No more than you meant to harm thousands of innocent people of whose very names you are ignorant," Esther said coldly. She must, she told herself, remember all those doomed ones, and remember, too, that Haman had brought this upon himself. Otherwise she might even find herself pitying him, suddenly so miserably abject after being so arrogant.

"What shall I do?" he whimpered, sensing the strength in her and instinctively seeking its shelter. "Your Majesty, if you will help, support, protect me now I will be your most humble and faithful servant to the end of my days."

"You are a stranger to humility and faith, Haman. I have seen your service. You are a servant who wishes to rule. I would not choose such a one. And why bargain with *me*? The King at this moment decides between us. He may choose you."

"He is displeased with me," Haman moaned. "My lady, unless you take pity and speak for me, I am doomed."

"I am doomed already. And many with me. How can I speak for another when I am one of those whose doom is written up in the market-place? I am a Jew. With what are *you* charged, Haman?"

The mockery in her voice struck like a blow and he gave a low wailing cry such as an animal in pain might utter. Rising from his place and reeling like a man struck with mortal sickness, he came to the end of the table where Esther was. There he flung himself on his knees. "I beg you, my lady, pity me. Speak for me to the King when he returns. Say you forgive me and understand that I meant you no harm!"

"And why should I lie thus, for you?" Her dislike for him increased as the scent of the heavy perfume with which he had drenched himself reached her, together with another odour, the strong unmistakable smell of the sweat of fear.

She leaned towards the other end of her couch and said:

"Control yourself, Haman. The King has not yet decided between us. I might as well grovel to you!"

162

"No . . . no!" he gasped out. "Your star is rising; mine sinks. I made a mistake this morning . . ." The memory of his confidence and assurance, his nearness to the realisation of a cherished dream, his bitter disappointment at hearing Mordecai's name, came over him and he began to sob. Past words, he began to claw at Esther with pleading hands, as a favourite dog will paw its master, seeking indulgence or notice. Blubbering and sweating and pawing at her he was utterly repulsive; she pushed his hands away and again leaned away from him, saying sharply, "Have you no pride at all?"

Meanwhile Artaxerxes' rapid progress had brought him to the end of the garden, to the place where the three fountains played into marble basins surrounded by small dark cypresses; a sickle moon hung low in the sky and a million stars seeded the night. The silence was broken only by the gentle tinkling splash of the water. Artaxerxes stopped; the quiet beauty of the time and place touched him with a great peace; the hammers ceased their beating on his brain. He began to think.

With an utter lack of any personal feeling, without shame, or anger, or surprise, he realised that he was a foolish, weak man. In a rapid, frank survey of his whole like — accomplished in a second of thought-time — he saw that, although he was King of Persia, the most revered and awesome figure in the whole of the world, he had hitherto been nothing but a gaily-dressed puppet figure whose strings had always been pulled by somebody else. Even when he had, on rare occasions, made a decision of his own he had invariably been prompted by temper, or pride, the desire for amusement, or the prod of a passing mood. Thinking thus frankly he found that he could credit himself with only one virtue, and that was physical courage. He was, he knew, a fine soldier, completely fearless, and in action, decisive and shrewd and resourceful; but life couldn't be all fighting, and in the ordinary matter of living he was a prey to anyone who set out to get the better of him. Courtiers, politicians, favourites, women . . . Only a moment ago, faced with the painful business of deciding between Esther and Haman, what had he done? Run into the garden as though by absenting himself he could escape from the need of making up his mind.

Well, he would now make up for it, calmly, decisively. Take Haman first. Haman had a talent for being amusing and entertaining; he said flattering things, and he said them differently. But on how many occasions had one deliberately shut one's eyes to the fact that Haman was coarse-minded, cruel, unscrupulous, not even fastidiously clean? And this morning Haman had revealed the full extent of his ambition. Haman's self-love was boundless.

Of Esther it was almost impossible to think so detachedly. The memory of the pang that had struck him when she had said, "You see, I am going to die," would intrude itself, bringing with it the sense of loss and panic and despair. He had realised at that moment how much he loved her, how very much she meant to him. But *now*, now he was thinking, not feeling; he wasn't giving way to emotion. So he forced himself to consider Esther coolly, detachedly. And the thing that stood out most clearly was that she had never attempted to exploit him . . . she was, in fact, the only person in all his experience who had treated him as an equal, as a human being with rights, and dignity . . . paying respects to his position, but at the same time looking upon him as a man. Artaxerxes saw in one mental flash, that if he were ever to rule his empire as successfully as he had led his army, the one person whose help and support would be valuable, was Esther. To everyone else he was King of Persia, a puppet figure to be pushed around, a giver of favours, a source of wealth, a subject of mockery (as with Haman), or even a matter of contempt (as with Vashti). To the others he himself, Artaxerxes, the man, didn't exist at all. To Esther the man was all-important; look how she had lain in his arms and kissed him and never, never once sought any favour for her family or her subject race. Esther, in fact, was a person, not a Jewess, or Queen of Persia, or one of a family, or one of a race, but a person, remote and detached, in her own right, and she treated him as such a person.

In a great calm Artaxerxes turned and began to walk back to the Queen's apartment. He meant, from this moment, to begin to rule his kingdom, with Esther's help. And he would say quite calmly to Haman that he disapproved of his behaviour, distrusted his ambition; and that as soon as all these iniquitous plans against the people of Esther and Mordecai had been withdrawn, Haman might himself withdraw from the Court. A modest estate, perhaps, and a small pension. After that, no more favourites, no more pullers-of-strings; just Esther and he, two people who loved and trusted and respected one another, working together. Victim — though he didn't know it — of yet another mood, but a mood which might eventually harden into character, Artaxerxes walked calmly back through the garden. The grassy lawn stopped short, some twenty feet off the Palace, and gave way to marble pavement. As he stepped on to it the sound was audible within the room.

Haman gave a kind of screaming moan and threw himself upon Esther in a paroxysm of terror. He took the upper part of her arms in his hands and shook her, trying by violence to command pity.

"He comes, speak for me, speak for me!" Esther tried to stand up, but he was kneeling upon the skirts of her robe and for a second she was pinned down. She had no notion of what decision Artaxerxes had made; she was aware of the full danger of her own position. She had offended him by attacking his favourite, and now she had made the deadly admission and the challenging accusation. It was quite possible that Artaxerxes might have decided in Haman's favour, and if so she wanted to meet her fate, the fate of all the Jews in Persia, with some measure of dignity. So she put her hands on Haman's shoulders and braced herself, pushing him away and making a more determined effort to free her robe and stand up. The gauze of her robe split and gave way with a thin shrill sound just as Artaxerxes pushed the curtains aside and stepped back into the room.

Haman, quite maddened by fear, grabbed at her knees and again she struck his hands away.

Artaxerxes, suddenly arriving, might be forgiven for misunderstanding the situation.

"You devil," he shouted, seizing Haman by his jewelled collar and jerking him backwards, "would you lay hands on your Queen?"

It was a very simple, natural question, but it told both Haman and Esther what decision Artaxerxes had taken. She was "Queen": Haman, "You devil." Haman fell, incoherent, almost insensible, upon the floor, and Esther, freed at last, stood up, gathering the torn folds of her robe together in her hands. Artaxerxes, master of the situation, shouted "Harbonah," and the chamberlain who had been taking supper in the ante-room, hurried in.

"Take this away and hang it," said Artaxerxes, indicating the prostrate body of Haman.

An instinctive, completely feminine cry of protest rose to Esther's lips; she withheld it. Thousands of men and women and children had been doomed to death by this creature; a tiger, an adder in the death throes, might be momentarily pitiable, but only a fool would spare them.

She stood, silent and dignified. Harbonah had been chamberlain in the palace for many years, and was incapable of feeling astonishment any more. He had seen the rise and fall of many favourites. No one had risen so quickly or so far as Haman; it was quite in order that his fall should be most sudden and complete.

167

"On the public gallows, my Lord?" he asked calmly. "Or on the new one recently erected on his own property?"

"Whichever is nearer," said Artaxerxes. And turning to Esther he asked anxiously, "Did he hurt you?"

"No," she said, shaking her head, while her eyes watched Harbonah dragging Haman away.

"He tore your dress," Artaxerxes said, putting an arm about her protectively and leading her back to her place at the table.

"That was an accident," Esther said. She wanted to put her arms on the table and lean her head on them and cry. We're all of us, however grand and dressed-up and titled, just men and women, she thought dismally, just masses of flesh and blood, very vulnerable. There are so many things in the world to hurt us . . . why must we try so hard to hurt one another? It's so sad; people hurting one another is the saddest thing in the world.

But she would not give way. Artaxerxes had decided in her favour, against Haman, and it was her duty to see that the favourite was not missed. If she had been the one to go to the gallows Haman would not have wept and been oppressed by the sadness of the world. Oh no.

"Perhaps I had better retire and re-arrange my dress," she said.

"Leave it," Artaxerxes said. "Let us resume our feast where it was interrupted." He sat down, rather suddenly, and reached for the wine, filled Esther's cup and then his own. And Esther abruptly remembered that the interruption had not just been a matter of

168

rivalry between herself and Haman. She gulped at her wine and then, in a voice kept deliberately light, said:

"I should feast better, my Lord, if I could first be reprieved."

Artaxerxes stared at her. "But of course," he said. "I was forgetting. Forgive me. All those orders must be cancelled immediately. What time have we?"

"Ten days."

"Oh dear," Artaxerxes said. "And I did want just to sit down and talk with you. Do you realise that it is a month since I saw you alone? But this is important. I'll assign it to Zethar . . . the only thing is he's old and slow. Send Zethar to me," he said to the hovering slave. "Esther . . . I'm sorry that I ever quarrelled with you over Haman."

Life had not schooled him to apologise and he felt awkward as he said the words.

"I was also to blame. I lost my temper," Esther said. And the child in him loved her for that frank and generous admission.

Zethar came in, grave, pompous, courtly old man. The years had, as he himself expressed it, "given him wisdom," but they had also set him into an immobile pattern of mind. Given a procession to arrange, a problem of court etiquette to solve, or an aspect of the law to be explained, then no one could be more valuable than Zethar. Of matters outside the Court he was woefully ignorant; he was secretly terrified of taking on new responsibilities, and he was lazy. He had also a most irritating habit of repeating, half as a question and half as a confirmation, one word or one phrase of an order. To a man in a hurry, as Artaxerxes was at this moment, it was exasperating in the extreme.

"Zethar, I want you to see about cancelling all those decrees that have been issued against the Jews."

"The Jews, my Lord? Exactly what orders were they?" asked Zethar, who was not a Jew, knew no Jew either as friend or enemy, and seldom nowadays stepped outside the palace boundaries.

"Orders were issued by Haman," said Artaxerxes, trying to be patient. "They come into effect in ten days' time, and the furthest point of the empire is ten days' swift travel distance away. For such places you'd better send young dromedaries. They cover the ground faster than horses, and can keep up speed for greater lengths of time. Set all the scribes to work at once and send off the notices to the further provinces first. Let a slave run to Haman's place of execution and bring back my seal ring . . . typical of him to go to his hanging wearing it! That will give you all the authority you need."

"Young dromedaries, seal ring — yes, my Lord. It shall be done, my Lord. May I ask one question? Where would the line be drawn between the further provinces and the nearer ones? I ask because of the distinction between the horses and the dromedaries."

"All that," said Artaxerxes, still striving to be patient, because patience was one of the virtues which he knew he lacked, and knew that he would need in his new role as good ruler, "can be learned from a glance at the map. The maps are in the record room, in the first rack on the right of the door. Astus would help you there.

170

One map, I know, is marked with the number of days' travel necessary to reach each province."

"The first rack on the right of the door," said Zethar. "One other question, my Lord. Would you wish the notices of this new decree posted as they arrive, or to await a day when they can go up simultaneously in each province?"

It was really a sensible question and showed that though Zether might be ignorant of relative distances, he understood the matter of procedure. But that question at that moment was too much for the patience, not of Artaxerxes, but of Esther.

"If I may speak . . ." she said, and then without awaiting permission, hurried on, "they should be posted at the first possible moment. Can't you understand, Zethar that everywhere there are men and women living, if you can call it living, under the sentence of death . . . as I was myself until a few minutes ago. Until you have experienced it . . . Let them know as soon as possible; use every possible endeavour to let as many people as possible go to their beds and sleep in peace, confident of their King's justice."

"At the first possible moment," Zethar agreed. But it was plain that he and haste were strangers to one another. Even now, when the tragic situation of so many people had been explained to him and he had in his power the means to relieve them, he stood, obviously wondering whether there were not some point that needed further explanation.

171

And to Esther, watching impatiently, occurred the idea that in a moment Artaxerxes would begin to miss Haman. The orders for the massacre, she was certain, had never caused Artaxerxes a moment's concern once he had said, "You see to it, Haman." Another idea ran alongside the first — if *I* could have the authority, how gladly, how quickly I would see to it all! Zethar is not the man . . . in all the Court there isn't a man capable of taking responsibility or wielding authority. Too much has been left to Haman. And then a third thought arose: it was Artaxerxes who had thought of sending the dromedaries — that was resourceful and showed a good sense of the situation; and Artaxerxes had remembered exactly where the maps were kept. Spoiled, easily bored, easily influenced as he was, he had the makings of a real ruler . . . if only somebody helpful were there to shoulder the more boring tasks, somebody completely unself-seeking there to wield the right influence.

I could do it, Esther thought . . . but I am a woman. I have to be his Queen, not his right-hand man. And then she thought of Mordecai.

She said softly, "Artaxerxes," and he turned towards her. "I'm sorry if I sound impatient, but I know, as you cannot, how these people feel. Counting the days, counting the mealtimes, almost counting the breaths. I've been doing it myself and I *know*. If they could have the news quickly it would be a personal favour to me."

"I know, I know," he said indulgently. "But Zethar," he looked at the old man and smiled to soften his next words, "hasn't had any experience in hasty matters.

However, if you will *try* to arrange this quickly, Zethar, I myself will help you. I will attend to the ordering of the dromedaries, and if you send Astus to me with the map I mentioned I will decide which provinces should be served with those and which with horses."

"And I will owe you my heart's gratitude," Esther said to her husband as Zethar ponderously went away.

"The trouble is that little administrative matters bore me," said Artaxerxes frankly. "It's a matter of training and upbringing I suppose. And I was trained to lead men into battle, not to see that their shoes fitted and their swords were sharpened. Somebody else did all that, and I still like to leave details to somebody else. Not," he added with a wry smile, "that many details can be left to Zethar. I must look out for somebody a little more active in body and a little less set in mind."

There were probably many men of talent and capability about the Court, Esther reflected; but Haman, for his own reasons, had kept them at a distance from the King. By to-morrow Artaxerxes would have chosen somebody; she had better speak now.

"My Lord," she said, "I know all vendors cry their goods in glowing terms, but I could recommend you a man, not young but very active, with an excellent mind and a passion for detail; entirely honest and unself-seeking and capable of taking responsibility and wielding what authority you choose to give him with dignity and integrity."

Artaxerxes laughed. "Add," he said, "that the man can read and write, is clean in his personal habits and invariably sober, and you have described a paragon, a creature as mythical as the unicorn."

"I'm deadly serious," Esther said. "And if you would have help with this business, if you want it done quickly and perfectly without trouble to yourself, you could send for him this evening."

"By the light of the sun, so I would; if the creature existed."

"He does! His name is Mordecai and he lives in the Street of Camels."

"But he . . . that is the man, Esther, whom I honoured this morning; the one who saved my life. What an extraordinary coincidence!"

"Hardly that," Esther said. "You see, he is my uncle — the one who brought me up."

"A duty of which, if I may say so, he made a most admirable job. No, no . . . I really mean that, Esther." A slightly rueful smile came across his face and made him look even younger than ever. "Out there this evening I came to the conclusion that you were the most real and the most nice person I had ever known, or ever should know. And I realised that I myself wasn't grown up yet. Perhaps this Mordecai . . . Mordecai could help bring me up, too." He laughed again, but there was a new underlying note in the laughter, and Esther realised that in yet another way this evening had marked a turning point in their lives. A man occupying the highest position in the world, surrounded by flatterers and self-seekers and sycophants all ministering to his vanity, who could admit that he was not fully grown up,

174

was not only a most lovable figure, but had in him the seeds of real greatness.

"We'll send for Mordecai," said Artaxerxes.

So once again Hatach despatched the idle little page to the Street of Camels, and this time he had the King's command to make haste. And before the young moon had made her circuit of the sky and was going down behind the pointed tops of the cypress trees Mordecai, in full charge of the measures that were to save all the men and women and children of his race within the bounds of a great empire, was busier and more serious than he had ever been in all his busy, serious life.

But in the Queen's apartment Esther, feeling that she had accomplished the task set her, and still a little fearful that Artaxerxes might suffer the growing pains of the soul and perhaps miss Haman's entertaining company, had set herself out to be amusing. And at the end of one burst of laughter Artaxerxes turned to her and said impulsively, "Esther, I do love you!"

"My Lord," she said, speaking as Zethar might have done, "this is very gratifying news. Reciprocal treaties are always the most satisfactory in the long run; and, you see, I love you too."

He leaned over and kissed her, and this time there was no shadow of a secret, no shadow of Haman between them. And Artaxerxes looked backward for a moment, reviewing all the things that happened since when? Since he had made ready for his feast of celebration. Vashti — all those women — Bigthana and Teresh — Haman — Esther.

"You know," he said gravely, "all this would make a story too."

"One day somebody will tell it," Esther said.